I Thirst

by
Gina Marinello-Sweeney

Cover photo of Perch Rock Lighthouse by Ray McBride
www.raymcbridephotography.com

Excerpt from "I Am Blest" by Chris Muglia

Excerpts from "Adoro te Devote"
Original Latin text: Saint Thomas Aquinas (1225-1274)
English translation: Father Mark Daniel Kirby, O.Cist., 2004

Scene break designs by Obsidian Dawn
www.obsidiandawn.com

Used with Permission. Thank you!

I Thirst

Published in the United States by Rivershore Books
9011 Pierce St. NE, Blaine, MN 55434
www.rivershorebooks.com

ISBN-10: 0615802125
ISBN-13: 978-0615802121

Printed in the United States of America

Dedication

To the best grandparents in the world,
Arthur and Vera Marinello

"He will give His angels charge of you, to guard you in all your ways. On their hands they will bear you up, lest you dash your foot against a stone."

Psalm 91:10-11

"My sheep hear My voice, and I know them."

John 10:27

Story Worlds

The Characters of I THIRST

Adriana   **Rebecca — Peter**   Chelsey   Cedric
↓

The Characters of INTERMISSION (written by Rebecca and Peter)

Monet — Antonio — Elise — Morena   Fred
↓

The Characters of "Muse" (written by the INTERMISSION cast)

Antonio   Patria   The Lighthouse Keeper

Prologue

The airy precision of a zipper's ascent was the only audible sound in the silence of the small room.

He bent down, firmly grasping the handle of the large, black suitcase near his feet. In a single movement, he was at the door, his hand reaching decisively for the tarnishing golden knob. Yet, now that he was at the threshold, he paused, turning back for merely an instant to focus his eyes on a small object that lay positioned toward the back of his desk. It was a brown, square frame holding a slightly battered photograph.

He blinked rapidly and turned the knob, taking a step out into the vast darkness of the quickly approaching nightfall.

Chapter One

Adoro

I entered the courtyard. Delicate petals bathed in amethyst and pearl surrounded me, bid me welcome. Even the sublime portal, half of a circlet the color of the first snow, knew their names.

My heart laughed and I spun around.

Left, right.

Back, forward.

Around and around

I climbed upon the top of the portal. It beckoned me forward like the call of a siren.

No, it was much sweeter.

It knew no poison.

It remained unstained, tainted by no defilement, tarnished by nothing.

It was free.

It was everything.

The portal grew…

Larger, fuller, deeper

I was in a palace of stone white. I moved to the rhythm of the music.

The Music.

It was here.

A music beyond music.

My vision blurred and, once again, I stood before the portal of flowery wonder. And, beyond the portal, was a great shroud of mist.

What lay beyond? I had forgotten.

All was lost.

No, all was found. The portal, once entered, lost the world behind it…

Baila.

Baila, Rebecca.

I opened my eyes to the sparkling sunlight of Easter morning and recalled.

Chapter Two

Te

It was the first day of Lent.
Ash Wednesday.

My eyes were fixed intently upon the Crucifix before me, silently praying a wordless prayer, as sweet waves of harmonic voices allowed me to travel to another dimension. In this moment, I did not know exactly what I was praying. Yet it existed, and I understood...understood without understanding. It was a thought, a feeling, a glimpse of the moment and, perhaps, the past and future.

I turned quietly to my mom, who was, as usual, singing along, her strong, triumphant voice holding close the words, "Let it be done." My heart smiled, and it was then that I saw the unfamiliar, solitary figure.

He was tall, with golden brown hair and eyes that brought color to the auditory waves of the choir. His shirt, white as the wing of a dove, shone brilliantly, a harmonic counterpoint to the deep azure of his tie. He was walking slowly, making his way from pew to pew with an offertory basket in hand. His countenance revealed an expression of peace—yet did not seem to be completely relaxed out of formality—and something else that I couldn't quite comprehend at the time.

When he neared our row of pews, I realized that I might have been staring, so I purposely averted my eyes slightly, pretending to be enthralled by the pews to my left. There was another reason, too, but I couldn't pretend to guess at its significance.

Despite my precautions, I soon realized that I was seated at the end of the row. *Great*.

Great? Why did it matter?

Yet I still turned, quickly facing forward, when, despite the much more dominant sound of choir music, I heard light footsteps gradually growing more pronounced. As I placed our envelope in the basket, a flash of gold appeared before my eyes, fluttering to the ground in a brief displacement of air. Yet I barely noticed, my heart still pounding strangely in my chest. I cleared my throat, turning again, in the most nonchalant manner possible, to my right. As I handed him the basket, his eyes met mine for an instant, an unreadable, yet penetrating, gaze illuminating his face. Then, he was gone.

I looked down at the floor, reaching quickly to retrieve the object that had flashed before my eyes.

It was a folded piece of paper, golden in color, that read, "For you."

In the Name of the Father, and of the Son, and of the Holy Spirit.

I closed my eyes as the coolness of ashes gently marked on my forehead became the Sign of the Cross.

The Sign of the Cross before which I now stood.

An outer sign of an inner grace.

And a prayer. An embrace.

And, once again, I was drawn into the Song, the Beauty surrounding me. Yet, throughout the rest of Mass, I also somehow sensed the newcomer's presence without seeing him. He had seemed, by my brief observation, to be seamlessly woven into the fabric of the church and, yet, there was, at the same time, something so entirely distinctive about him, something that marked him as very different from the rest of the parishioners and, truly, from anyone that I had ever encountered. The thought crossed my mind that I was just nervous, and a vision of my reluctance in high school to introduce myself to an exchange student from Spain flashed before my eyes. I had watched with fascination this singular figure, unknown and mysterious, from a distance. Yet I somehow understood that this was something more.

At the end of Mass, I put on my jacket and grabbed my purse, still feeling, despite myself, the need to appear busy. I looked at my mom. She seemed to be searching for something in her purse. I couldn't help but smile. My mom's purse was a filing cabinet, a collection of a million years…only without any form of labeling system. I noticed with amusement a movie ticket from two years before.

And, since I'm waiting…

I sat down again, opening the note that I had retrieved from the floor.

There was a single word within, type-written in a flowery font like the words on the front:

Intermission.

My eyebrows furrowed in confusion. *Well, that was random…*

"Rebecca!"

I looked up to observe a short, dark-haired girl waving frantically from behind the last row of pews in the center aisle. Her greeting had only been a loud whisper at most, yet her hands indicated more extreme sentiments. A contagious smile lit up her face.

It was Adriana, my best college friend…no, my best friend since the tenth year of my life.

I quickly stashed the note in my purse, tapping my mom lightly on the shoulder.

"Hey, Mom. I'm going to talk to Adri for a sec."

My mom nodded distractedly, still fumbling with her purse. I walked towards the back of the church and soon reached Adriana. She was still smiling, more widely than usual.

"Okay, dude, you look like you're on a mission."

Adriana continued to grin and bobbed her head excitedly. I must have given her a weird look because she was barely able to stifle a fit of laughter.

I lifted a finger to my lips. "No hyenas in church. Of course, you could just *say*, 'LOL'. "

That didn't really help matters; the two of us automatically burst into laughter. I grabbed Adriana's hand like a young schoolgirl, and pulled her towards the back section of the church. I glanced backward for a second, hoping that my mom would figure things out. I had left my cell phone in some undetermined place in the house.

I stopped before the door, dipping my finger into the small stone basin before me. I only had a moment to touch the coolness of the holy water to my forehead before Adriana made an attempt to drag me out of the church. An elderly usher, upon observing us, cocked his head to one side as if to establish the view that aliens had taken over the planet. I smiled apologetically as Adriana whisked me away, but not before I saw the beginnings of a smile form in the man's large, gray eyes.

Okay, so maybe they were nice aliens.

I closed the door lightly, amazed that I accomplished this much with Adriana's strange, yet not particularly anomalous, mood.

There is an unspoken pact between best friends that stipulates the following:

To induce laughter, all you have to do is *look* at your partner-in-crime—even in the absence of said crime.

A few days earlier, Adriana and I had been browsing books at the local library. I happened to turn around and look at her...and that was it. The man who "loved to laugh" in Mary Poppins had nothing on us. And the man browsing the books next to us had nothing but a vindictive nature.

And today, on Ash Wednesday of all days, and in front of church, of all locations, that was exactly what happened.

I rolled my eyes. "You should be excommunicated."

"Oh yeah? Because I'm the one who celebrates the doorknob's birthday? Surely that defies some sort of moral standard."

"Not at all. The doorknob is one of the most important inventions yet," I responded dryly.

Adriana snorted and the two of us burst into laughter once again. After the sugar in the air had dissipated, I eyed Adriana again with mock seriousness.

"Enough of this. What's up with the drama y misterio?"

"Your tendency to randomly insert Spanish words into everyday dialogue...or *monologue*, rather..." Adriana smiled mischievously.

I glared at her, pretending to ready a sword in the air.

"What I was saying," Adriana continued, brushing away my invisible weapon as if it were a fly, "is that that very tradition of yours connects to the matter at hand. In fact, it almost *answers* your question."

Her eyes twinkled with amusement, seeming to take pleasure in my complete and utter confusion.

(Which, of course, she did.)

I rolled my eyes again. "Thou speaketh in riddles."

"I hate Shakespeare."

"And I hate loud, discordant so-called 'music' defined so appropriately by the term 'heavy metal rock'," I pronounced, enunciating each word deliberately and with clear distaste.

Adriana burst into laughter again, seeming to enjoy a private joke.

"Well?"

"*Well,*" she said, "it so happens that there's a salsa dance at the park gymnasium the Friday after next at precisely 8 PM. Wanna go? We could grab Chelsey and it would be a girls' night out."

She smiled sweetly, demonstrating her expectation of my reaction.

The local "park" was ironically as much defined by "inside" activities as outside. As a child, it had defined my every summer.

I stared at Adriana, this time in true disbelief.

"Since when have you been interested in dancing?"

"The last time I checked, *I* wasn't the one who tripped over a glass container of sugar that I had myself dropped...after, of course, having received several bruises from an attempt to retrieve a flip-flop that had somehow ended up in the sink."

"I suppose the contents of that unfortunate container were symbolic?"

"Possibly," Adriana snorted.

"Anyway, dude, what's up with the dance? What's the *real* reason behind your sudden interest?"

"Does there have to be a 'real' reason?"

"Yes."

"Okay. My favorite member of Rising Potatoes took up an interest in salsa dancing and will be present at the event."

Adriana always seemed to be obsessed with obscure bands. This was the loudest and most obnoxious of them all.

"Nooo!" I screamed, mimicking Luke Skywalker to the best of my ability.

Several people turned around, eyeing me with curiosity…and either slight amusement or annoyance.

I cleared my throat. I did not frequently exhibit my insane tendencies in public. I turned back to Adriana. The smile of amusement touching her lips had reached her eyes.

"I love to dance, whether I'm good at it or not," I lifted an eyebrow like a Vulcan before continuing with a glare. "So, despite my reservations as to the guest list…"

Adriana snorted again.

"…I'll attend the event."

"Good. I'll notify Chelsey of your decision."

"She already knows? I must say, I'm…offended. Unlike her, you've known *me* since fourth grade."

"Dude, she's in my Saturday art class. You're not."

"I was just joking."

"I know."

"Anyway, I'd better get going."

"Me, too."

"See you on Friday at 8, then?"

"Indeed."

I heard a familiar step behind me.

"Hi, Mrs. Veritas!"

"Hi, Adriana! Heard that you got a new job...how's that going?"

"Well, it's a *job*, but it's going well," Adriana replied with a smile.

"She's in Adriana Sanctuary," I said, grinning at Adriana, "all those antique CDs."

Adriana put on her best stuck-up Nineteenth Century English Noblewoman expression.

"I'll have you know," she retorted with assumed haughtiness, "that we have an assortment of selections to entice many different tastes. All varieties of heavy metal music CDs."

"A *wide* variety of musical selections for sure," I muttered, grinning.

Adriana pretended to ignore me and continued, "From classic caveman metal..."

She stole a mischievous glance at me.

"...to Rising Potatoes."

We both burst out laughing. My mother eyed us with the "aliens taking over the world" expression that we had received many times earlier. Minus the curiosity, that is. She had long given up trying to understand our many inside jokes.

"Well, girls," she eyed us warily, "time to go."

I gave Adriana a hug. "Parting with such sweet sorrow, dude."

"Farewell, dude."

Our constant switching between two seemingly opposite dialects—that of a bygone century and that of the current century that my mom would rather disregard—was likely whiplash for the random observer. For my mom, it was something far from out of the ordinary…she just thought that we were weird.

I grinned.

Ciao.

Chapter Three

Devote

"Stage 2 Sleep."

I yawned.

Chelsey stole a glance at me, grinning. Her thin blonde locks flipped back into place as she refocused on her notes. *And the doodling surrounding them.*

I grinned back and refocused my attention to the front of the room.

I loved psychology. I really did. But the chapter on Sleep just reminded me of what 8 hours divided by 2 equated.

Wisps of thin, gray hair floated on top of Dr. Everson's head. His penetrating blue eyes were full speed ahead, caught in the excitement of light years of psychological study.

Someone snored.

Dr. Everson's eyes addressed the class, amused.

"Ah, class," he said in that booming voice of his. "Some of us have gotten too much into the new chapter. Perhaps we will re-adjourn later…after everyone has completed all four stages of sleep."

A chorus of laughter and smiles ensued.

"Dr. Everson is such a cool professor," Chelsey whispered as she quickly began to pack up. "Only one hour gone, one hour of freedom coming up!"

I nodded, putting my notebook in my backpack. I felt sort of bad for that brief interchange with Chelsey earlier. Dr. Everson was an easy-going guy, but I respected him a lot. Well, at least *I* hadn't snored.

I followed Chelsey out of the room.

"Wanna hang out here?" I pointed to some nearby benches.

"Sure."

We sat down. I turned towards Chelsey and noticed that her bright green eyes beamed with excitement.

Oh no, not another friend on a mission.

I didn't have to ask.

"Oh my gosh, I have news!"

"What's going on?" I was pulled easily into the excitement. "Oh my gosh" was a mind-altering phrase.

"Aaron texted me. I think this is good, right?"

She flipped open her cell phone, pressed a few buttons, and eagerly threw the phone into my waiting hands. I read the words on the screen:

u changed my world, girl.

"Well?" She snatched the phone back the instant I saw the last word.

"Sounds good," I nodded encouragingly. Aaron was the subject of half of our conversations, so it got a bit old. But I felt for Chelsey. Since his college was located in another city, she only saw him about once every two months. And, even if she did act like a teenage drama queen whenever she talked about him, I wasn't convinced that she wasn't madly in love with him.

"Really?" Chelsey's eyes addressed mine dubiously.

"Really," I said more enthusiastically. "It's really sweet. I guess it just sounds too much like…a text."

"Well, yeah, you can't always have Shakespeare on a cell phone."

We laughed.

"'Y-o-u' is only two more letters."

"True. Whatever. He's so gorgeous and sweet and smart and *everything*."

I smiled, "I'll have to meet him one day."

"Yeah."

We sat in silence.

"I miss this," Chelsey finally said. Heat from the sun shone brightly on her tanned face. "I could lie on a beach and feel the sun on my face all day."

"The rain has gotten a little old," I agreed, gazing quietly above. "Usually I prefer a little cooler weather, though. But I love the beach."

"Oh, me, too. Sometimes I would go with friends

and just sit back and watch the waves…for hours."

"Exactly!"

It wasn't often that I found someone who wanted to meditate on the waves of the sea. Everyone else just wanted to surf…or be seen.

In that instant, I yearned for the poetry of those riddle-filled, yet comforting, waves, the aroma and soft caress of an ancient sea breeze, and fairy dust beneath my feet.

The sea was a paradox.

"The semester will be over soon," I said, encouraging myself as much as Chelsey.

"Not soon enough! I have so many papers to write!"

Chelsey and I commiserated over our piles of homework assignments for a while, and then it was time for her next class.

"Later, Rebecca. See ya at Golden Spoon tomorrow!"

"Bye, Chelsey! See you then!"

I was alone.

And yet the great blue sky was above me and my eyes thirsted for its words.

I found myself staring at the heavens. It had me hypnotized. *Hypnotized* by something that we see every day…yet hardly ever *truly* see.

I gazed at it for an eternity, absolutely absorbed and truly fascinated by how *blue* the sky could be.

Blue. So many people would call the color blue the most perfect, the most pure, yet I had always preferred an enigmatic crimson or delicate pink…and, for eyes, deep, soft brown. Yet there was something different here…a native blue like the ocean, a certain peaceful yet challenging and mysterious magic that called upon those to listen who would. Simply azure, completely and everlastingly blue, *eternal*.

The true azure.

I heaved a great sigh. I felt like a child, a snapshot of my beaming brother testing the waves for the first time at the beach. Sure, there was a brush of white clouds, splashed seemingly sporadically over the great surface, yet the background was too bright, too brilliant, to be subdued. It was too clearly defined a pattern on this canvas of the Divine.

Something like this has probably been said a million times in a million different ways…but how often do we take the time to appreciate it by enacting the words ourselves? I thought.

As I tilted my head to observe an observer, a vehicle making a little trail of white in the sky, I caught sight of Dr. Everson and two other psychology professors. They were walking nonchalantly to the left of the nearest building.

A great opportunity for one of them to whisper in the ear of another. "Let's observe this strange girl in her natural habitat."

I smiled and returned to my own study.

As I was sitting—eating my lunch with more relaxation than I had experienced in a while—I heard a slight rustling behind me and turned.

It was a small rabbit, as white and fluffy as an cumulus cloud, chomping blissfully on green shrubbery. I watched, mesmerized, by the simplicity before me. I watched, pleasantly surprised by this slight interruption in the pattern of natural silence, even though, as the member of a campus so full of wildlife, my sense of wonder might have expired long ago. As it was, I often passed a family of ducks on my way to class.

Yet I was, by full definition of the word, *surprised*.

My lunch ended up lasting half an hour.

When you're eating lunch with a friend, it can go on forever as you continually chat. A bystander would have said that I was eating alone.

But I was not. I was sharing a meal with God…and many elements of His Mighty Creation.

It was a prayer.

I entered the library to complete my Spanish homework, newly baptized in the goodness of life, unable to find anything displeasing.

And then I wrote. And I wrote like I had never written before, filled with an ecstasy of spirit that provided instant inspiration. My four hours of sleep doubled, and I walked peacefully and awake to my next class two hours later.

Thank you, God. Thank you for this beautiful world that I really needed today.

Chapter Four

Latens

"Déjà vu! That's what it is!" I exclaimed.

I had been pacing back and forth across the small area near our table at Golden Spoon. Chelsey and Adriana eyed me with confused amusement.

"Huh?" Chelsey questioned.

Adriana chuckled. "Need we ask?"

"Yes." I returned to my seat with a great flourish and leaned forward eagerly.

"If you're planning on saying it, hurry up. If not," Adriana said, her eyes twinkling, "it's best that I return to my frozen yogurt without fear of choking."

"The frozen yogurt that you undoubtedly selected

because you knew that I gave up chocolate for Lent."

"Precisely. As your friend, it is my obligation to challenge you."

I shook my head with a smile before feigning an exasperated sigh.

"Really, Rebecca, what were you talking about?" Chelsey brushed a strand of hair from her eye.

"This place is…giving me déjà vu," I said, suddenly losing my humor as I became lost in thought.

"Well, you've been to Golden Spoon plenty of times," Adriana laughed, before taking another spoonful of Chocolate Raspberry, "it's not *that* odd."

"No," I insisted, "it's not about Golden Spoon." My friends stared at me skeptically as I searched for words. "I mean…it's not that…it's déjà vu to lunch time at our old high school…when a bunch of us would sit by the library wall facing the Quad to eat."

"That's not déjà vu," Chelsey said practically, "it's the place that has to seem familiar."

"Whatever you want to call it," I waved my hand impatiently. "It's here."

"Okay." Adriana took my comment with calm acceptance. She was used to my strange outbursts. While we were often comrades on the same wave link, we also had our own unique brands of insanity that would take the most precise microscope to uncover. Yet the differences united us as much as the similarities.

"Well, you *could* show a little more interest," I rolled my eyes and grinned.

"What I'm interested in," Chelsey interrupted

eagerly, "is more details on this new usher at your church. Adriana was telling me about him."

What a convenient change of subject.

But I soon forgot my "déjà vu" with this one.

"Oh, the tall one?"

Adriana rolled her eyes. "Don't even try to pretend that you didn't notice."

"I'm surprised, Adriana...since when were you a giggly boy chaser?"

"I am *not*," Adriana said defensively, fiddling with her spoon. "Chelsey was asking if there were any cute guys at St. Vitus'. I said that I didn't really notice, but that the new usher might be her type."

"Okay, okay, sorry, Adriana." I made a :P face. She proceeded to bestow upon me the same honor.

"So, is he cute?" Chelsey asked me.

I paused for a moment.

Was he? How would I describe him? And I had only seen him for an instant.

"He intrigues me," I said slowly, "for some reason. But, you know me...I like the 'tall, dark, and handsome' type. This guy is nearly blond."

"'He intrigues me'," Chelsey repeated with a laugh. "Sounds like you, Rebecca. Weirdo."

"Ha, ha. Weird and proud of it!"

"Tall, dark, handsome...and *mysterious*," Adriana mused, her eyes dancing. "Don't forget about that last essential item on your list!"

"Yes, that, too," I answered as something caught in my throat.

"And don't forget that this one *is* tall, if blond."

"Uh huh. Whatever."

"So, he's up for grabs?" Chelsey inquired, leaning forward.

Adriana rolled her eyes. The words "Rising Potatoes," which were splashed sporadically across her shirt, seemed to agree.

"What happened to Aaron, Chelsey?" I raised an eyebrow in fun, but part of me was slightly annoyed. I had my celebrity crushes based on looks. But, for some reason, it bothered me in the real world.

Chelsey blushed. "I was just joking. Besides, I can still *look*."

Adriana stood up. "Ready to go, dudes?"

"Sure," I replied quickly, pushing in my chair. I was grateful for Adriana's choice of intermission.

Chelsey eyed us both. "Dudettes."

"Less catchy," I replied with a smile.

Chelsey shook her head and smiled. "Let's go."

As I bit into a juicy tomato, my mom walked into the room.

"Hola," I greeted her, before taking another bite. Homegrown tomatoes were my weakness.

"Hola," she replied, opening the refrigerator.

"Mom, peanut butter...do you *have* to?" I complained as the smell of sticky mush filled my nostrils. It was another 'weakness' of mine.

"Peanut butter is very healthy, Rebecca," my mom reminded me with a grin. "You might want to have some today."

"No, thanks," I muttered, picking up a white napkin to dab at my lips. "I'll pass."

"Suit yourself," she said, continuing to lick a coated spoon as she sat down.

I looked at the sliding glass door that led to the backyard. It was first a theatrical gesture in defiance of the sight of peanut butter, but, as I continued to maintain my stare, it turned into a gaze.

The heavens were now brushed lightly with a hint of pink mist, a mist seemingly held in suspension by a majestic swirl of purple. Two nearly identical images of the windows in the front door overlapped in reflection upon a bushy tree, darkened to forest green in the dim light. Yet, while the replica on the left remained colorless, its counterpart on the right reflected the colors above.

The phone rang.

Startled, I moved out of my seat to take the call, but my mom had already relinquished hers. I sat back down.

I turned back to the door, hearing a word or two indicating that it was my father. But I did not really take note of the conversation until my mother's voice began to change. It became softer, barely distinguishable.

"How long?"

I quickly got up from my seat. I looked inquisitively at my mom, but she did not notice. There was no mistaking the worry lining her face.

"A week? When do they expect him to…leave the

hospital?"

The pause in my mom's nervous words pounded in my chest. *What was going on?*

"Okay, don't…worry about anything. Just drive home safely. I'm sure that everything's going to be all right," my mom smiled, as if she had forgotten that Dad couldn't see her comforting gesture. But her voice had taken on a degree of confidence, whether or not she felt it. For that, I was grateful.

"Mom?"

I bounded over as soon as the receiver was put down.

As Mom stood in the doorway, it seemed as if she had aged a decade. While the delicate weaving of gray, black, and white was seen by most as a mark of the elderly, the strokes of my mother's hair had always had the opposite effect on me. It was like the beauty that could be found on a rainy day…or, perhaps, the aftermath of the rain that wasn't an "aftermath" with the usual connotation of the word, but the fresh, life-giving air and light rain drops that seemed to magnify the smallest leaf. It was a cloud of…everything. And it was Mom.

Yet now the stereotype of gray hair was present in her great brown eyes that were so often joyful. When she opened her mouth, I could tell that she was trying to calm us both down with her words.

"Dad just called to say that Monsignor McGregor is in the hospital."

Chapter Five

Deitas

It was the first Sunday of Lent.

The week had passed in such a blur of unreality that it was hard to believe that it was Sunday once again.

Father McGregor had become like a father to Dad when his own father had died of cancer. At the time of the tragedy, Dad had been only fourteen.

I closed my eyes and felt my surroundings, felt beyond my surroundings.

God, please, heal Monsignor McGregor. Please. My dad can't take this. He loves him so much. And, even though I don't know him as well, I do, too. *I do, too.*

Come, Holy Spirit.
Lord, You are my Shepherd.
Our Father Who Art in Heaven
Guide me.
Guide us all.
Amen.

I felt an arm around me. It was Mom. She looked at me and knew.

And then the music came and washed over me with sweet sympathy. It beckoned me and I drew closer, held in a tight embrace.

It turned into an outstretched hand, holding a sacred Communion host.

May almighty God bless you…the Father, and the Son, and the Holy Spirit.

I crossed myself, hugging God close.

I crossed the aisle, following my mom and a crowd of fellow parishioners to the back of the church.

"Hi, Josie!"

My mom had caught sight of an old friend. They crushed in a close embrace. I smiled in greeting. As they began to talk, I realized that I had neglected to pick up the weekly bulletin. With a quick nod in their direction, I walked over to the nearby "bookshelf" of church flyers.

"Hi, there."

I turned swiftly and came face to face with the new usher that I had seen the week before.

He was smiling. It was not a wide, brilliant smile, but a small, thoughtful creasing of the lips. His large eyes took me in, a question and a statement all in one.

He was wearing a white dress shirt and a blue tie, like last week, and stood, tall and calm, before me. Calm, yet, once again…*something*. Reserved?

I didn't have time to think further. He was waiting for a reply.

"Hey! You're new here, aren't you?"

"Yes."

I felt stupid and he had answered my stupid question with an obvious answer. I searched for words, but instead clumsily put my hand forward.

"Rebecca Elizabeth Veritas." I laughed nervously. "I probably should have said that earlier." I felt my face turning red.

And why had I mentioned my middle name anyway? It sounded so formal.

"Don't worry about it," he said, a wider smile surfacing. "We've only been here for a few seconds."

"Peter Joseph Asturian."

His hand gripped mine firmly. I withdrew my hand with a surprised smile.

His smile turned into a grin. "Sorry. That happens all the time. I probably should have learned by now to avoid killing people's hands."

I laughed, suddenly feeling more at ease. "'Tis okay, my hand remains alive."

'Tis? Okay, that was a good sign. If I could get into ancient dialects this early, then maybe I wouldn't act like an idiot during the rest of the conversation.

Peter laughed, a low chuckle. "Glad to hear it."

I turned at the sound of a group of people walking toward the community room, often used for meetings, as well as extra space during Mass, with assorted musical instruments.

"Huh, I wonder what that is."

"They're getting stuff ready for Family Day." Peter's eyes still followed the line filing into the room.

"Family Day?" I asked curiously.

Peter turned back to me, his hazel eyes bright with some secret joy. "It's a Canadian celebration. When I came to the United States a few weeks ago, I asked if there was a similar tradition at St. Vitus Catholic Church. As there was not, I recommended it. It's a celebration of the importance of the family and its values, which also ties into the Church."

"Oh, you're from Canada?"

So, the exchange student thoughts were not too far off.

"Yep, born and raised. Ever been there?"

"No, at least not physically."

Peter surveyed me with a curious expression.

I laughed slightly. "I mean to say that I love Canada…well, Prince Edward Island, without having been there."

"Lucy Maud Montgomery fan, eh?"

It was my turn to be surprised.

"How did you know?" I asked, pushing a wisp of hair distractedly from my eye.

"Hot tourist spot. Prince Edward Island *is* Lucy Maud Montgomery to so many people."

*His voice had a nice, different quality to it. Quiet, thereby seeming to confirm my earlier suspicions that he **was** a bit reserved, yet not so quiet because it was so…**firm**.*

*Firm and **solid**.*

"It is to me," I smiled. "A lot of my childhood memories are on that island. *Anne of Green Gables...Emily of New Moon*...everything. It made me obsess over lighthouses." I felt like I was rambling. "And *Avonlea*'s one of my favorite TV shows," I finished.

"Avonlea? I was visiting relatives on the old isle some years back when they filmed part of that."

"No way!" I exclaimed excitedly. "That is *not* fair!"

Peter grinned, seemingly amused at my outburst. "It was great. I got to meet the cast and everything."

"We are no longer on speaking terms," I stated firmly.

It sounded exactly like something that I would have said to Adriana.

"Even though we have just begun to talk," Peter grinned.

"Exactly."

I heard someone clearing his throat. We turned to see the elderly usher who had seemed entertained by Adriana and me the week before. He surveyed us with another amused expression.

"Just a sec, Cedric," Peter said, answering his unspoken query.

Peter turned to me, his eyes penetrating mine. "It was great meeting you, Rebecca," he said, shaking my hand again, this time with a less powerful grip.

"Likewise."

"See you next week, Rebecca."

"See you next week."

I stood there for a moment, watching Peter follow

the older man into the small room to the left of the community room known as the usher's closet. It was a picturesque sight; I found myself reminded of the scene of a shepherd guiding his flock of sheep. But, in this particular instance, I wasn't quite sure which individual was the shepherd…and which a member of his flock.

It was almost as if time had frozen.

I grinned at the overly dramatic comparison that had presented itself in my mind, and turned to look over my shoulder. My mom was still talking in the exact spot where I had left her. I went over to her and waited silently, smiling again in greeting at Josie.

Then I went back to get a copy of the bulletin.

Chapter Six

Quae

I put my backpack down on the sofa and sighed. I wasn't the least in the mood for homework, but it had to be done. I took my physics book out of my backpack and walked over to the table.

"*¡Hermana!*"

I turned around and instantly rolled my eyes.

My brother was standing behind me, grinning widely, with arms outstretched theatrically. Rebellious locks of fiery red hair fell across his forehead.

"What's *up*?" he bellowed.

"Actually, today, it *is* the sky."

I had once again meditated on the heavens that

afternoon.

Alexander scrunched his eyebrows together. "Weirdo."

"I know that which you do not." My eyes widened as I leaned towards him dramatically.

"Freak."

"And happily so."

"Hasta la vista."

"Good. I *do* have homework to do." I waved a physics worksheet in his face.

"Lame, lame. Goodbye."

My brother salsa danced away…and then it was just me and Einstein.

$E = mc^2$.

Huh, something that I had actually known before enrolling in this class. Physics hadn't turned out to be as bad as I had thought it would be.

At least I wasn't learning about how plants breathed. I preferred observing their poetry to studying their logistics.

After I finished the relatively easy math problems for physics, I walked down the hall to my room. On my desk was *The Chronicles of Narnia* soundtrack. I flopped onto my bed and reached over to put the CD in the player…

I was in a great forest. Branches of emerald green surrounded me, as I tried in vain to brush them aside. I stumbled on an unseen root, falling to the ground. My knee stung, but I pushed myself up impatiently, barely noticing the pain.

Something drew me forward, urged me onward, insisted

that I continue. It was as if nothing else mattered except this journey.

I finally broke free of this tangled web of green. I found myself in a clearing, a small brook bubbling happily against tiny, chiming pebbles. Zephyrs of wind gently caressed my face as I smiled at the picturesque scene.

Then something went wrong. I couldn't see it with my eyes, but I felt it…deep within myself.

I looked at the brook, and then at the green outskirts. Nothing had changed.

But suddenly it was as if the air had been stolen from my chest. I struggled to breathe as the forest whirled around me…until it was nothing but a deep and overwhelming blackness.

I jumped up. "Only the Beginning of the Adventure" was still playing softly on my CD player. Relieved, I lay down once again. It was one of those rare moments in which I was consciously aware of my own breathing.

Before I had asthma, that is.

But this wasn't asthma. What *was* it?

It had seemed so real. And yet I had never been in a forest before, though the literary world had brought me there so many times.

Time for further thought quickly expired as I heard my dad calling the family to dinner.

Yet, as I slipped off my bed and walked down the hallway, my thoughts were still lost in that great, tangled forest.

"Rebecca?"

I dropped my fork in surprise. I heard the resounding clinging noise against my empty plate as I looked up. My father eyed me quizzically.

"Sorry, Dad. I was thinking of something. Did you have a question?"

"Well, yes. For the last billion minutes or so."

"Sorry." I looked up at my dad. His brow was creased in slight annoyance, but the eyes that surveyed me were more amused than anything else.

Thin spectacles were placed precariously, almost comically, over a small, cheerful nose. Deep blue eyes of the sea sparkled from behind them, as brilliant locks of red shone above them. When I was a little girl, he would always protrude his glasses farther down his nose and make faces so that my photo smile would be genuine. He was a first grade teacher at the local elementary school, beloved by all, yet a unique individual...unlike the rest.

My dad was the reason for The Annoying Yet Amazing Anomaly known as my brother. Well, obviously, my mom had something to do with it, but all the credit for the hair went to my dad. And I firmly believed the saying that red hair only increased certain personality traits.

Mom interrupted my idle thoughts. "Your dad wants to know whether you need a ride to the dance."

"Nah, Dad, I'm fine." I became more alert. "I can carpool with Chelsey and Adri."

Dad nodded offhandedly.

He seemed so cheerful. *But I could tell.*

I jumped up and threw my arms about his neck. "Wanna play Crazy 8's?"

"Don't want you to have nightmares over your defeat," Dad grinned, lifting an eyebrow.

Truly grinned.

I pushed in my chair. "Oh yeah? We'll see about that, *cheater*!"

I ran to my room, once again a little girl in search of playing cards for her dad.

Mi papá y yo.

Chapter Seven

Sub

It was the second Sunday of Lent.

"Rebecca."

I turned around.

It was him. Of course. Who else would it be?

"Hey," I greeted Peter with a smile, walking towards him.

"I thought we were no longer on speaking terms...?" he raised an eyebrow.

I grinned. "Weren't you listening to the sermon at all? You know, about forgiveness?"

"Yeah, but I wasn't quite sure if you were. You seemed rather...lost in something today."

So, he had been watching me. No wonder I had felt self-conscious during Mass the first day I had seen him. Yet, today, in this moment, it did not seem to bother me.

His voice had softened, his face growing thoughtful, the amusement robbed from his words. Yet his eyes searched mine, seemingly preoccupied. My face warmed at his concern, yet it soon burned from a different source as I felt a stab in my chest.

"Oh, maybe," I laughed uneasily. "A lot on my mind."

Primarily Dad and Monsignor McGregor. Yet I felt uneasy about something else, and I wasn't quite sure *what.* My upcoming physics exam? No, it was something far, far deeper. I had realized this as I sat quietly in my favorite pew during Mass.

And, as I had gazed at my surroundings, at the muted, yet triumphant, colors splashed in joyful serenity over the immaculate stone floor, at the profiles of my fellow parishioners bent in prayer, and finally, up above, at the flickering lights held in a soft gray ceiling like chandeliers in an ancient palace, I realized that my thoughts had been transferred to Someone Else.

Peter nodded, accepting, yet I seemed to detect something in his eyes. He knew that I had not said everything, yet had chosen not to pursue it.

I was grateful.

I knew that I couldn't explain it. It was, after all, something that I did not entirely understand myself.

But I also suddenly felt that I owed him an explanation.

Or, at least, *something*.

"And sometimes," I said quietly, my voice speaking for me, as if I were listening to a recording of it, "I can find Him when I am so lost in my thoughts."

His countenance suddenly relaxed, and his eyes held mine. I found myself unable to turn, to look away. It was like looking into a whirlpool that circled on and on yet never allowed you to get dizzy.

"I understand," he said softly, maintaining his gaze.

And, in that instant, I knew, beyond the comprehension of words, that he did.

"So," I broke through the silence deliberately, "how was your week?"

Although the atmosphere had become one of peace, the...*intimacy* of that peace had invited nervousness.

I regretted my words as soon as they left my mouth. They only solidified my embarrassment.

Yet, it could have been worse, I argued with myself.

"Good," he said cheerfully.

If he had noticed, he made no show of it.

"Too much homework, though," he added, annoyance evident in his voice.

I readily grasped the opportunity for a new turn in the conversation.

"Same here!" I moved my hands emphatically in agreement, "it just piles up! I wish professors didn't feel to need to rush through things right before Easter vacation."

"Yeah," Peter nodded.

There was another lapse of awkward silence and I silently shouted at myself, wondering if I could have avoided such a moment by saying something else.

But that didn't make me talk either.

"You said, 'Easter vacation'," Peter spoke again, looking at me thoughtfully. "I don't hear that a lot lately, even at SHU. It's…refreshing."

"Yeah, I've never been one to go for politically correct nonsense."

Paul nodded vehemently in evident exasperation.

"But SHU?" I continued. "What's that?"

"Sacred Heart University. My college."

"Oh, did you just start there this year?" I asked.

"Yeah, when I moved out here. I'm a sophomore, though…turned 20 just before I left Alberta."

"Nice!"

I had been about to ask him his major, but, much to my surprise, he quickly spoke again, with hardly a second to spare after my pathetic attempt at conversation.

"So, what do you do for fun?"

The statement seemed so absolutely…*random* that I had to try hard to keep a straight face.

"Um…" I began, still somewhat taken aback, "I like to write…stories, but more often poetry."

I felt my face burning, as it often did when I was taken by surprise. I also felt like a five year old describing her favorite things.

"Right."

I looked up, suddenly realizing that I had not been maintaining eye contact, but, rather, fiddling with my cell phone, a practice that I normally condemned.

Peter Joseph was nodding his head, as if in

confirmation of a known fact.

My face must have shown the surprise that I had felt, for Peter began to chuckle, his eyes surveying mine almost scientifically. It was a deep, rich laugh, startlingly old for a twenty-year-old yet, at the same time, appropriately youthful.

"Okay, so, who asked the question…and who gave the answer?" I demanded in mock, yet extremely curious and confused, accusation.

"I can recognize a partner-in-crime a mile away."

I blinked and only had a moment to laugh before another emotion demanded precedence.

"You're a writer, too?" I blurted out eagerly, unable to contain my excitement. The five-year-old had definitely taken over both my mind and my mouth.

"Yes, I suppose you could say that. But, for me, it's a passion, not The Passion."

I could hear the capital letters in his voice.

"I don't think it's possible to have writing as anything less than The Passion," I said slowly, emphasizing the case of the letters as he had. "It's more than just a profession or hobby…it's a way of life."

"As cliché as that might sound," I added with a laugh, faintly disappointed at the likelihood of having made my life sound like a commercial slogan.

I looked up, and my eyes were once again drawn into an intent gaze. Peter was neither smiling nor frowning, yet his eyes were far from indifferent. They seemed to penetrate deep within me, yet, at the end of the long tunnel, my mind's eye detected approval.

"You're right," he finally said, not averting his eyes

for an instant, "and, as for clichés, they're an illusion. When you think about it, anything could be considered a cliché. It's when you really bring truth to something that it becomes original...which may," he smiled wryly, "itself be considered a cliché."

I laughed in surprised delight. It was a natural laugh, yet internally I stared in disbelief.

Was this a Canadian thing? To have a second conversation be so...well...I searched for the word...so **intimate***?*

No, it was a Peter thing.

"I think you're right," I finally said, eyes still fixed in the same position, as if in obstinate refusal to lose a staring contest. "It's like," I searched for the right word, "coincidence."

He jumped on it immediately. "In what way?"

He hadn't seemed to read my mind about that one.

I grinned.

"That's for me to know and you to find out," I said, basking happily in immaturity.

"So, I'll know one day?"

"Perhaps."

"But you're not going to tell me when you shall...*disclose* this information, are you?"

"Nope."

He shook his head, smiling.

Peter seemed to be *really*, truly, and honestly interested in knowing.

Most people might have maintained a slight curiosity...before casually dropping the subject, never to be remembered again.

But I had a feeling that Peter wasn't going to forget it. In fact, as I finally broke eye contact and looked away for a moment, a smile beginning to weave its way across my face, I realized that it was more than a feeling. I just *knew*. And this knowledge, although seemingly insignificant, gave me a strange satisfaction.

I turned back to my new friend.

Back on Earth, Peter was shaking his head, a grin unreservedly alighting his countenance.

"Rebecca," he said, "you're...odd."

"Thank you," I replied haughtily with a quick toss of the head and a glint in the eyes.

Yet Inner Rebecca wasn't quite sure how she felt about this. *What exactly did he mean by that?* I wondered.

Despite what I had thought to be a well-executed statement, somehow Peter had caught that non-existent visible trail of my inner doubt.

His eyes took in my question as if I had said it aloud.

"I meant it as a compliment, Rebecca," he said quickly, his voice now softer.

Yes, he did. He had said "Rebecca" before, too. That had somehow made a difference.

"Odd is a compliment," he continued, his eyes twinkling, "whereas weird is an insult."

"I'll keep that in mind," I grinned.

Truly grinned.

[Exit.]

Chapter Eight

His

"So…what exactly are they doing anyway?"

I half-sighed, half-laughed. "For the one who proposed the event, you sure are clueless."

Adriana stood, posed as if ready to engage in battle. Unlike her temperament, her long locks of raven black hair were held together in a tight braid. She wore a royal purple baby doll dress, joined at the top by a golden circlet. It would all have been so normal had the words "Rising Potatoes" not been splashed sporadically over the front by a bright orange marker.

All around us, flashes of color swirled in perfect harmony with the rhythm of the music.

Baila. *Dance.*

And, here, we were, at the center of this masterpiece, *ruining* it. I suppressed a laugh, as this thought suddenly reminded me of another anomaly: my grand entrance during a performance of "Macbeth" that I had attended the summer before. With the play about to begin, I had discovered that my dad had dropped me off near the stage area. I had searched desperately for a less conspicuous place to enter. But, alas, I had soon found that the area was neatly enclosed by an uncompromising gate. There was no possible entry point…with the exception of a small bridge toward the center of the arena. As soon as my feet had left the bridge, an army of old rushed towards me from the left. I immediately lost my desire for time travel and was not aware of the play until the second act.

I brushed a tendril of hair from my eye. I had selected, after some deliberation, a simple, spaghetti strap dress of a flowered print. I had almost borrowed Chelsey's high-heeled black shoes—made by a famous designer that I had never heard of—but had thought of the sugar container and decided against it. I wore casual, off-white sandals, which probably went better with the dress anyway. I let my dark curls fall naturally into place.

"Okay, Adriana, I'm no expert, but watch this."

Out of the corner of my eye, I noticed Chelsey walking back to us, freshened from a water break. She immediately began to dance in a free-style sort of format, the folds of her short, light blue dress billowing slightly about her. I slowly modeled the salsa steps, which Adriana readily copied.

"Good job," I said approvingly, as I watched Adriana quickly catching on. "Now, a little faster."

Satisfied with Adriana's progress, I turned slightly and soon lost myself in the dance.

I entered the courtyard. Delicate petals bathed in amethyst and pearl surrounded me, bid me welcome. Even the sublime portal, half of a circlet the color of the first snow, knew their names.

My heart laughed and I spun around.

Left, right.

Back, forward.

Around and around

I climbed upon the top of the portal. It beckoned me forward like the call of a siren.

No, it was much sweeter.

It knew no poison.

It remained unstained, tainted by no defilement, tarnished by nothing.

It was free.

It was *everything*.

The portal grew…

Larger, fuller, deeper

I was in a palace of stone white. I moved to the rhythm of the music.

The Music.

It was *here.*

A music beyond music.

My vision blurred and, once again, I stood before the portal of flowery wonder. And, beyond the portal, was a great shroud of mist.

What lay beyond? I had forgotten.

All was lost.

No, all was found. The portal, once entered, lost the world behind it…

Baila.

"Rebecca?"

I jumped. The music murmured and quickly faded, a flute's final journey.

Adriana was waving a hand spastically near my face in half-amusement and, perhaps, like me earlier, half-annoyance.

"Um…water break?" I rubbed my eyes.

Adriana snorted. "Um, try, *final* 'break'. The 'baile'," Adriana pronounced the word with a dramatic accent, "is kinda over, dude. But we may obtain some refreshing water if you so desire."

I still felt a little dreamy, like I often did when departing from the shuffling images of a movie theater screen. But, unlike the post-movie experience, I now felt wholly *awake*…or, if not awake, *alive*.

"Water, girls?"

Chelsey handed each of us a sealed water bottle. Her cheeks were flushed, her hand flicking back a strand of hair.

"I love to dance!"

Chelsey threw her hands into the air and swiveled her hips to illustrate her point.

I unscrewed the cap and took a sip.

"Mmm," I murmured, "The Search for Delicious."

"Huh?" Chelsey's eyes questioned me.

"Just another attempt by Rebecca to connect an

everyday occurrence to the literary world," Adriana pronounced with a grand wave of the hand.

"Hey," I protested, "there is a clear connection between the author Natalie Babbitt and water. In this book in particular…" I cleared my throat upon observing my friends' facial expressions. "But there is no need to spoil the plot."

"Book nerd." Adriana's eyes addressed mine with a grin.

"And happily so," I retorted, feigning an offended sniff. "But, you know, since we're here…" I added with a mischievous grin, "We might as well delve deeper into the symbolic nature of the liquid. From the beginning of time, the image of water—"

"Water is love, baby. Let's share the love."

I turned my head to find a young man with a complex Mohawk grinning openly at us. A golden earring hung rebelliously from one ear below bright, green eyes completely surrounded by eye liner. He stood, posed ostentatiously with a cup of water (or so it appeared) in one hand.

"So nice to meet you," I called as I pushed my friends through the door.

As the door slammed shut in squealing protest, I thought I heard the unfortunate anomaly calling, "But I didn't even get your name!" in the wake of a resounding eruption.

"Interesting fellow," Adriana lifted an eyebrow.

"Yes," I grinned, "even a bit too *eccentric* for you."

As Adriana prepared to tackle me, Chelsey nodded in apparent agreement with my last statement.

"He might have been cute without the Mohawk, though," Chelsey suggested.

I sat down, turning the pages of my notebook in search of a blank page, in the dim light of my room. The arrival of nightfall had invited leafy shadows to play hide and seek in the glass reflection of the window. I smiled as one of these mischievous shadows crept across the page in a midnight dance.

I was seated at the great mahogany desk built by my grandfather, the rest of the family fast asleep.

It was Friday, the end of a rather unremarkable week, a week with enough homework to keep you from having much fun but not so much as to distinguish it as one of the unusually horrific.

I picked up my pen, not knowing what I would write, yet aware that something would be written. I closed my eyes for an instant and then began to paint a picture in my own way.

I trace the pathway
To an ancient palace
Lined with the shimmering waves
Of seaside glory.
Tumbling after one another
They race, beckoned
By yonder shore.
The highest tower
Of grey-worn fortress

The rosy blush
Of an early morrow
Of yesterday's today.

I trace the walk
Of its smallest garden
I weave my way
Through the sprinkling
Of golden crown's last flower
Tiny footprints of seagulls
Leading a wanderer astray
When crossing each other
In a mixed confusion
Of scrambled understanding
A maze of orderly disorder.
A snowy white sail lingers
Woven in wisps
Of cool, heavenly air
Alit by the brightest torch
Of sentinel's caress
Held in the chalice
Of a half-forgotten world.

I traced my pen back to the top of the page and wrote,

"Yesterday's Chalice"
By Rebecca Elizabeth Veritas

I had not been to the beach since last summer, yet the picture in my mind was as vivid as if it had been a part of yesterday.

And, of course, it was.
I put down my pen and gazed into Eternity.

Chapter Nine

Figuris

It was the third Sunday of Lent.

It was the end of Mass, and Father Muñoz was reading the weekly bulletin announcements. A deep purple chasuble covered his linen alb, vestments that symbolized the sorrow and penance of the Lenten season. He was older, yet younger; although wisps of gray were scattered among his brown locks, his large, dark eyes, deep and clear, held an almost ageless understanding.

"Family Day, based on a Canadian custom, will take place two weeks from this Monday at 1:30 PM in the parish hall. It will honor the timeless family traditions and values that we as Catholics celebrate."

I instantly smiled. Peter's voice had been etched with such pride when he had spoken about the celebration.

"May almighty God bless you…the Father, and the Son, and the Holy Spirit. Amen."

The closing hymn triumphantly sounded. I told my mom that I could be a while and that Adri was going to pick me up afterwards to hang out.

Mom nodded and I waved as I made my way to the back of the church.

Peter was not where we had met on the previous two occasions.

Really, Rebecca…do you expect him to be there all day? I asked myself dryly.

I peeked around the corner at the usher's closet. *Maybe…*

I breathed a sigh of relief. He was there, calmly organizing some papers, perhaps next week's bulletin. There was something in the casual, yet formal, way in which he moved that was…

"Hey, Rebecca!"

My thoughts took an intermission.

Peter was standing at the threshold of the room, leaning lightly against the door. He smiled, a smile which reached his eyes and did not seem to be without curiosity.

I jumped.

"Lost in your thoughts again?" Peter proposed, lifting a "curious," Spock-ish eyebrow.

"As usual," I grinned. "So, how's it going?"

"Good."

"Okay, so…I have a question."

He chuckled. "Ask away."

"Since we have, thanks to your randomness, covered what I do for fun, may I inquire as to what you do for work…*o sea*, study?"

"*O sea*? So, your major is Spanish?"

"Wrong!" I waved my hand in a gesture of grandeur.

So, his mind-reading abilities were stalled for today.

"Good guess, though," I added. "It's my minor."

He cleared his throat. "Well, English would have been my first guess, Poeta."

"Wrong again!" I proclaimed triumphantly. "It's psychology."

"Ah," he nodded, "that works, too."

"Huh?" I raised an eyebrow. "Must you always be right?"

"No, but you're a writer. By definition, that's a psychologist in disguise." His lips began to curve once again into a smile. "And you seem to have an added sense of curiosity that would prove useful in that field of study."

I was stunned once again. *Where did he…how…*

"Philosophy," I suggested.

"Minor."

We both began to laugh. It was a long, hearty laugh that we shared, and, when it reached its finale, I wiped moisture from my brow.

"Okay, then…what? I give up!"

"Elementary education."

"High five!"

He laughed, and held up his hand in anticipation. Yet, as our hands met, I noticed a mist form over Peter's eyes, a cloudy mist that seemed to carry him in two directions. I caught my breath. His face had become paler, almost drawn.

I pulled back and attempted a smile. "That's great. I love kids."

"Me, too," Peter said quietly. He was no longer facing me, but the adjacent wall.

There was a heavy silence broken only by my rapid breathing. I stood, waiting, *wondering*.

Peter suddenly turned towards me once again. The color had returned to his face.

"You could come up with something more random," he said, crossing his arms.

A challenge.

"Okay. What will you be doing tomorrow at precisely 1:23 PM PST?"

"Helping out at religious ed. Next question."

Huh.

I had wanted to follow up that question with another, but continued, as if I were a talk show host short on time.

"Any siblings?"

Peter paused. "One brother."

Do your parents live here?"

"No, they remain in Canada."

His voice had softened…and a strain of sadness seemed to line his face. My heart instantly went out to him, and I said nothing.

After a moment's pause, I continued.

"Their...profession?"

"Now *that* question will receive a more random answer." A smile once again appeared on his face, and I realized that I had been holding my breath because I suddenly began to breathe again.

"I won't be offended if you laugh."

"No, I wouldn't," I said earnestly.

"They own a shop of exotic jam."

I laughed.

He grinned, and now it was his turn to raise an eyebrow.

"I meant...no offense," I babbled. "It sounds like an awesome job, but, at the moment, it just seemed kinda—"

"Random," he finished, still smiling. "And I know. No offense taken."

"But...*exotic* jam?" I persisted, "like what?"

"Ever heard of Duku jam?"

"Star Wars?"

"No, I assure you that it is from *this* planet. Duku fruit grows on a small island...I forget which one." His brow creased slightly in concentration.

I nodded. "Just exotic? Or do you have the regular plum and apricot, as well?"

He chuckled. "Yeah. I just like to shock people with that 'exotic' part."

"Well, you certainly succeeded here," I retorted, readjusting the purse strap that had attempted to escape from the spill of laughter earlier.

There was a slight pause, and then, suddenly, Peter's face lit up. He leaned forward slightly, in an eager, almost casual, gesture that seemed, for some reason, to be uncharacteristic of my knowledge of him thus far.

"I have a proposal," he announced, watching me closely as if in anticipation of a reaction.

He did seem to enjoy studying me. Wasn't *I* the psychology student?

"All right," I replied. "What is it?"

"We should write a story together."

I almost fell backwards in excitement.

"Dude, that is such an epic idea!" I exclaimed.

Peter lifted a finger to his lips in amusement. A few parishioners still remained in the church, knelt in prayer.

I repeated my last statement in a whisper.

"I gathered as much," he smiled.

"So, when do we start?" I asked eagerly.

"Whenever. I have homework and other stuff to do, but, otherwise, I'm pretty much free. And soon homework won't even be a worry."

"Okay! Same here! And..."

I paused for a moment, a snapshot of the first day that I saw Peter materializing in my mind. "I have the perfect title for our work."

"Oh?"

"Intermission!"

From the expression on his face, I gathered that Peter was alternating between Pantomime "What the heck?!" and Pantomime "What planet did you come from?" before finally recomposing his face with a slight smile and the words, "Intermission it is, then."

I felt the need to explain.

"You see," I began, watching another smile grow slowly across Peter's face, "it is quite possible that, in a hypothetical scenario, a given person—let's call him Subject A—was sitting during the intermission of a play, the thought dawning upon him...'Hey, that should be the name of a story!'"

"Indeed? Is that what happened to you?" Peter raised an eyebrow in expectation of the answer.

"Not exactly."

"...Curious."

"I have a perfectly logical reason for this!" I protested with a smile.

"I do not doubt it," Peter folded his arms across his chest, his smile having reached its peak. "And it's an interesting title. Nevertheless, it struck me, at the moment, as rather—"

"Random," I finished, grinning ridiculously.

He laughed. "Exactly."

"Which is why," I began mischievously, "it shall center around a shop specializing in none other than Duku jam!"

It was then wise to make a quick and quiet exit.

www.yahoo.com
Connecting, website found.
I impatiently typed in "lighthousekeeper45" and

my password.

I had one email.

I grinned.

It was from <u>canadianpeter522@aol.com</u> .

I eagerly clicked on the message.

It was Thursday. For the past three days, I had hurriedly—yet, as a result of my hopeless perfectionist tendencies, *thoroughly*—finished my homework prior to engaging in a sort of email 'chat' with Peter about our newly-conceived project. We had decided to let the "intermission" part of the story figure itself out. In the meantime, we began to develop a plot and characters…in the hopes that the meaning of the title would emerge out of all of this.

The Duku jam idea stayed. However, like that of Peter's parents, it was not just a Duku (which, by the way, is from the island of Terengganu) shop, but a jam shop specializing in exotic fruit…and exotic customers.

Is it bad to fall in love with a character that you created yourself? A bit vain?

I wish I could have seen Peter's face when I suggested the character "Fred."

Fred was an elderly anomaly of Irish heritage who always appeared with a conical straw hat of the Japanese style perched on his head. It was said that he was a retired sea captain, although no confirmation of that fact existed and nothing else was known of him. Every Wednesday, he ordered pounds and pounds of some rare jam—probably Duku—and nobody knew why. *And* he had a pet parrot.

To this, Peter replied:

> This is AMAZING. There is a Fred of
> sorts who is a regular customer at
> my parents' store. Haha. He doesn't
> own a pet parrot, though...to my
> knowledge.
>
> Can't wait 'till Monique meets
> Fred!! :D

Monique was a ballet instructor who quit her job to work in Pudding Palace, which was next door to the jam shop. She often visited the shop, forever critiquing the quality of its products and the presence therein of rather eccentric visitors, such as Fred. Whenever this happened, Fred naturally just looked at her and smiled as she rambled.

Naturally. I smiled. We were already getting to know our characters pretty well.

Peter and I had developed Monique's character together, although most of our characters thus far were devised individually and *then* brought together. I noticed that Peter's characters were generally less eccentric than mine. I considered mentioning my observations, but held back. However, whenever such thoughts came to mind, a prediction that the response would have been " :D " followed.

:D. I had quickly learned that Peter's favorite emoticon seemed to be that "big grin." I was somewhat surprised at his usage of Internet lingo; it seemed almost contradictory to his nature. Yet I soon found that it suited him. I also found it to be personally

satisfactory. It helped me to "see," to more easily visualize his reaction, when he was not physically present. I always imagined his grin when I "read" that emoticon in particular. *Ridiculously large and subtly philosophical.* Whenever I saw it, I pictured that unique smile of his slowly forming at the corner of his lips to finally spread across his entire face.

And, whenever I saw it, I couldn't help illustrating it myself.

Sometimes I would also send Peter a cyber "hug." He never disregarded it with isolated detachment in his response, but he never returned it either. It could have been forgetfulness, it could have been nothing at all, yet I still wondered as to the reason. *If the reason existed.*

lighthousekeeper45@yahoo.com writes:

```
Okay, putting it all together,
Peter. :)

~* Jam Shop Staff Bios *~
```

Elise
- ❖ 22; long, brown wavy hair; brown eyes
- ❖ youngest member of jam shop staff
- ❖ in college; jam shop = summer job
- ❖ major crush on Antonio - willing to say anything to

defend Antonio, but determined
to not make it obvious;
however, in reality, her
efforts stand out and often
make little or no sense
- limited knowledge of Spanish
sometimes leads her to
misinterpret what is said by
Morena (ie. idioms) and become
offended when thinks Antonio
is insulted

Antonio

- ❖ 26; curly black hair; deep
  brown eyes
- ❖ was born in Italy, but moved
  to the United States when he
  was eight; has a slight accent
- ❖ songwriter; playing the violin
  is his Passion
- ❖ enjoys sci-fi and poetry and
  fancies himself a writer of
  both
- ❖ exceedingly stubborn; does not
  take well to criticism

Monet

- ❖ 32; straight blonde-ish/light
  brown hair; dark blue eyes;
  mustache
- ❖ disgruntled former French
  chef: restaurant was closed
  due to bad economy
- ❖ major critic of everything;
  prides himself an expert in
  all things: VERY hard to
  please

❖ jam shop "veteran" - feels
   that he is in charge
❖ always gets into arguments
   with Antonio

Morena
❖ 45; straight black hair; brown
   eyes
❖ moved from Venezuela 15 years
   ago; learned English through
   Shakespeare
❖ very intelligent; strong
   personality
❖ an interesting mix - enjoys
   sitting back and laughing at
   ridiculous scenes of the shop
   resulting from the antics of
   its eccentric employees, but
   also very respectful of
   artistic efforts made (ie. in
   story writing together) that
   "entran su corazón"
❖ sometimes comments on said
   amusement in Spanish, a
   language of which only Elise
   has some knowledge

The Owner
❖ remains unnamed
❖ rarely seen in story and,
   thus, almost legendary

I read the new email, a compilation of our character descriptions, becoming, at the same time, lost in my own thoughts.

As we wrote the story, digression naturally

occurred…and we began to talk about ourselves, about our own lives. The follow-up question that I had wanted to ask Peter during our little "20 Questions" after Mass materialized when I finally asked about his work in religious education.

canadianpeter522@aol.com writes:

> I love it. Kids make me feel...alive. They are what is truly genuine in this world.

lighthousekeeper45@yahoo.com writes:

> I agree completely, Peter. You know, I was thinking...maturity is so often considered to be synonymous with 'adult'. But I truly feel that maturity may be defined by the ability to be both an adult and a child.
>
> But, in a world where 'adults' murder children, that definition may never become mainstream.

canadianpeter522@aol.com writes:

> There is always hope. This world has become so corrupt, yet it is still a world that was created by God, the image of Perfection. Therefore, goodness still remains.
>
> And, in the end, good always

vanquishes evil. :D

lighthousekeeper45@yahoo.com writes:

> You're right, Peter. It's just so
> easy to get discouraged and
> frustrated with everything that's
> been going on.
>
> My family and I get involved in the
> pro-life cause whenever we can.
> During the Christmas season, we
> help with a poinsettia sale that
> supports the local Life Centers. If
> you're still in CA next December,
> you're welcome to help! :D

canadianpeter522@aol.com writes:

> It is so great, Rebecca, that you
> and your family are activists...on
> the *right* side. :D I would love to
> help out if I am still in the U.S.
> then. At this point, that's the
> plan.
>
> On the more serious side of Duku
> jam—during Lent, a percentage of
> its purchase goes towards the pro-
> life cause upon request.

lighthousekeeper45@yahoo.com writes:

> Dude, that's amazing! So, right
> now, your parents are doing that?

```
Seriously, though, that's
wonderful. :)
```

I instantly regretted pressing the "Send" button upon recalling Peter's sadness last Sunday when the conversation had turned to his parents.

canadianpeter522@aol.com writes:

```
Yeah, I miss helping with that.
```

Chapter Ten

Vere

"¡Desgraciado!" I bellowed.

My opponent fell to the ground in a heap.

The applause sounded. I grinned and took a bow as Chelsey stood up and wiped off the seat of her pants.

I glanced over at Señora Castellano, who smiled in a mixture of amusement and approval.

Chelsey smiled at the audience, and we returned to our seats.

"Página 106," Sra. Castellano instructed the class as she returned to the front of the room.

I turned rapidly to the indicated page, still caught up in the excitement of the skit.

Skit. Like a play, only shorter.
My brain soon caught up with my thoughts.
Intermission. A short break during a play.
A play within a play. A story within a story.
I couldn't wait to tell Peter my idea.

The angular velocity of the hands of the classroom clock was exceedingly slow today. I finally gathered my belongings together after what seemed an eternity, and walked toward the door at the end of Lecture.

Thank God it was Friday.

Thank God physics lab came before Conversación y Composición.

As soon as I got home, I threw down my backpack and hurried to the computer. I waited impatiently for it to wake up. Finally, I was able to type in my account password, and then the subsequent code on my email homepage.

lighthousekeeper45@yahoo.com writes:

```
Peter,

I have an *idea*. I don't know why
it didn't come to mind before. It's
all b/c of Spanish class...well,
```

> okay, to make a long story short...
>
> Since it's "Intermission," what do
> you say to having a 'play within a
> play', so to speak? Oh...does that
> sound too cliché? If clichés
> existed, I mean...

I knew that Peter came home from school around the same time that I did. He had told me before that he would then often check his mail after a quick snack. It was entirely possible that I would hear from him soon.

In the meantime, I might as well have a snack, too.

I ran to the kitchen, rinsed off an apple, and began to chomp.

Chomping took too long.

I rushed to the computer and refreshed the page.

No answer.

I chomped and rushed.

I sound like such a stalker.

1 email.

He was online. I knew it!

I eagerly clicked on the message.

canadianpeter522@aol.com writes:

> Even if clichés existed, it
> wouldn't be one.
>
> Bravo!

It was a good thing that I had not gone for the chomp/rush combination effect.

What would the play be about?

canadianpeter522@aol.com writes:

> And each scene that is not part of the play within the play takes place at the jam shop...

lighthousekeeper45@yahoo.com writes:

> Or in the adjacent park where strange things are known to happen...

canadianpeter522@aol.com writes:

> ...in those moments in which the principal characters gather after important stuff like school and work.

lighthousekeeper45@yahoo.com writes:

> So, we have two plays, one within the other. Yet, perhaps, at the same time, one *is* the other.

canadianpeter522@aol.com writes:

> Two pieces of a single puzzle that fit together.

<u>lighthousekeeper45@yahoo.com</u> writes:

```
But, dude, that doesn't make sense.
```

<u>canadianpeter522@aol.com</u> writes:

```
It does to us.
```

A scene from "Muse"
Written by Antonio

Antonio surveyed his surroundings nervously.
Colorless chandeliers attached to long strands of what closely resembled icicles, shed no warmth. Yet there was a strange/eerie/odd light emanating from it like the reflection cast by swimming catfish.

Monet: CATFISH?!?!? CATFISH?!?!? And what are all these slashes??? This is a PLAY! We need BRACKETS, not indecisive little scribbles!

Elise: Adorable!

Morena: Me encanta…but maybe we could skip the catfish part.

From the look of it, he was standing in the large chamber of a great castle and he had no recollection of his journey hence. Nor did he understand why he was carrying a basket filled with 50 jars of Duku jam.

Monet: Ha, ha…very funny. Can we TRY to have a serious play??? No magnetic wombats, no flying hyenas, no catfish masquerading as samurai, and, MOST CERTAINLY, *no* Duku jam! And TOO MANY ADJECTIVES!!!

Elise: I think it's cute! We do have a jam shop after all!

Morena: Let's leave it for the intermission…

At the back of the grand chamber, Antonio caught sight of three large doors, each a different color: pink, blue, and green.

Monet: What is this…*The Dating Game* ????

Elise: How cute! I hope he goes in the pink door!

Morena: ¡Qué chévere!

As he drew closer, instinctively believing/feeling that the answer to his question lay beyond one of those doors, he found that each door was not simply a solid color, but that an intricate design covered the surface. On the pink door, swirls of floral splendor crept delightfully across its surface.

Monet: From The Dating Game…to
   Shakespeare?!?!?? And TOO MANY
   ADVERBS!!!!!

*The blue door, upon closer inspection, appeared to not be
a door at all, for it was nearly transparent like the surface of
a turbulent sea/calm lake. The third door was a jungle, and
Antonio wasn't quite sure if the monkey on the front right
corner was real. Thus, Antonio edged toward the altogether
too pink door with much reluctance.*

Monet: Change in writing style…AGAIN!!!!!!

*Yet, as he moved his hand, eyes half-shut in disgust,
towards the magenta doorknob, he suddenly heard a great
rumbling. One by one, each of the twelve chandeliers —*

Monet: What…did ANTONIO stop to count the
   chandeliers?!?!?!?!??!?!?!?!?!?

—shook with a vengeance.

Hi, **Morena** here…Monet, um, took an
   intermission.

Elise: He needed to eat some jam.

*The last thing Antonio remembered was an icy blast—so
cold that it burned—and he was thrown, sprawling, into*

Door #1...The Blue Door That Appeared Not To Be A Door At All.
    BOOM!!!!!!!!!

Monet: You already convinced us that you were
        juvenile. This was not necessary.

Morena: He's back.

Elise: I think it's adorable and artistic!

I looked over the emails with a smile. *It was a start.*

    Peter had suggested that, in order to 'get to know our characters' better, we could start with a scene of the story written by a member of the jam shop troupe and the others' comments on the piece. I readily agreed, selecting "Antonio" as the first writer with Peter's approval. Since I had chosen the name of *Intermission*, I let Peter pick the name for this one. He selected "Muse" after some deliberation, which seemed fitting. We switched off, writing a paragraph of the story at a time. At the very end, we wrote the comments, often interspersed by laughter that surely was carried far across cyberspace.

Chapter Eleven

Latitas

socalgurlforevah@hotmail.com writes:

```
Rebecca,

I hate Spanish. Sra. Castellano is
cool   and   all,   but   it's   still
annoying.

I'm freaking out about the final!!
Do you want to study together?!

Love,
Chelsey
```

I rubbed my eyes. I had to remind myself that everyone had different tastes. But I still couldn't understand how someone could *hate* such a beautiful language…a language that I personally found to be much more expressive than English.

lighthousekeeper45@yahoo.com writes:

```
Chelsey,

No te preocupes. Sounds like a
plan. Tomorrow after psych?

Love,
Rebecca
```

I responded to a "dude"-filled email from risingpotatoeswarrior@yahoo.com about the declining quality of superhero villains and was about to log off my email account when letters in bold suddenly appeared on the screen.

A new message.

A new message from canadianpeter522@aol.com.

Peter.

```
Hey, Rebecca!

Remember that Canadian holiday I
was talking about, Family Day?
Tomorrow we're having a meeting to
plan the event. Interested?

Peter
```

Sing a new song.

Delicate footprints circled around and around in a softly traced maze. I breathed in the scent of the deep crimson rose petals before me, and a glimpse of a thought suddenly surrounded them.

"I have an idea!" I announced, as Peter stapled some pamphlets together.

"Yes?" he turned towards me with a wry smile.

"Well, you said that Heritage Day is the same day as Family Day, right?"

Peter nodded, his eyes waiting, curious.

"Well," I began, "I must confess that I did a little research."

Peter smiled, but said nothing.

"And your own province of Alberta in which Heritage Day is celebrated is known for the symbol of the rose. Roses make me think of the Virgin Mary. And it's *Family* Day. What about the Holy Family?"

"And sheep!" Peter exclaimed, his amusement turning quickly into excitement. "The Rocky Mountain bighorn sheep is another symbol of Alberta...*and* it's associated with Heritage Day!"

"The Lord is my Shepherd!"

"Exactly! GMTA!"

"GMTA?"

"Great minds think alike!"

I grinned.

"So, kinda like a St. Joseph's Day procession?" he

suggested.

"Only different," I finished.

Peter eagerly turned to his right, invigorated by the sound of Ideas. "Tom!"

A tall, young man with sandy brown hair and dark green eyes looked up from a stack of recipes. Of course, no celebration could be complete without culturally-connected food. Culturally-connected, *yummy* food.

As Peter explained our idea to Tom—I, fervently interrupting him with details—I could have sworn that I heard a low, quiet chuckle from somewhere in the vicinity. I turned around.

The elderly usher with whom I had never spoken—verbally, at least—who always seemed to watch me with amusement, was standing by the rose arrangement where I had positioned myself earlier. The light wrinkles in his face creased slightly as his lips curled into a smile.

I hadn't even noticed that he was in the room.

I turned back to Peter. He did not appear to notice the old man's contribution to the conversation and was still discussing details with Tom.

It was nearly evening. Peter had told me—rather, *ordered* me—to take a break when I confessed that I had forgotten to eat lunch. And, I finally complied. I watched Peter from a distance as he moved back and forth, talking with his hands. He was explaining a game that he had recently developed, a sort of Capture the Flag concept with a Canadian twist of red and white.

I soon finished my 'lunch' and turned to my slightly-beaten writing notebook. It wasn't my fault that the thing was dead, I reminded myself; it was simply the unavoidable fate of any item that I brought everywhere with me.

The pages parted instantly to the front, where a lost pen had taken refuge. Affixed to the front cover was my "Yesterday's Chalice," now typewritten.

I was suddenly drawn to the words that had come to me a few weeks earlier, and they to me. *We were one.*

I must have been staring, soaking in my poem, for some time, for it wasn't until I heard the soft staccato of footsteps that I remembered where I was.

Peter stood silently behind me.

Peter. *Naturally.*

"May I read it?"

He stood close, but at a slight distance. I knew that it was out of respect.

His eyes became soft as they approached mine, taking in my hesitation.

"If you're not ready, it's okay," he added gently.

If *you're* not ready. Not "if *it's* not ready." For some reason, his choice of words made a difference.

No, I was not ready.

I handed him my notebook.

 "It's really not that good," I said quickly. "I mean, I'm not the best writer anyway, but it's not the best…of my worst. Well, I mean…it's not exactly the worst of my best either, but…"

I let my words trail off. Once again, I was *rambling*.

He had not yet opened the notebook and was simply smiling into its cover.

"Which is why it's attached to the front cover...almost," his smile broke into a grin, "as if for inspiration." His hand moved to open the notebook.

He had caught me red-handed.

"Well, I do like to look at it sometimes before writing," I mumbled.

A small smile played at the corner of his lips. But it was soon replaced by a more serious expression as his eyes concentrated on the notebook before him.

"Poetry," he commented.

"You don't seem surprised."

"It was obvious," he said simply. And then I saw that he was absorbed in another world and I knew to say no more.

There is nothing more nerve-racking than waiting as someone reads your writing. The reader becomes the videographer, zooming far, far into your heart and soul, unveiling every inch and corner. The writer remains a wary observer at the mercy of the reader, clueless as to how he might react. The writer is exposed, laid bare; her innermost thoughts and feelings are revealed in a potentially scathing moment of vulnerability. I trusted Peter so fully...in a way that I could not explain. For that very reason, it mattered so immensely. To actually *tell* him what I knew he had already often seen in my eyes was to allow him to enter a new dimension in that world. And it *mattered*. It really, truly mattered.

At some point in this span of time—as these thoughts and others waited in the silence of an approaching night—I saw his head rise, slowly.

For a moment, his eyes were covered with a misty haze, thoughtful, yet lost in some reality that he called his own. It was like a fog filled with clarity, a paradox of thought. But soon they cleared, and a quiet smile filled them.

He handed me back the notebook.

"That was…beautiful," he said simply.

His eyes penetrated mine, and I knew that his words were sincere. Yet I couldn't help blurting out, my face reddening with a ridiculous grin,

"Really?"

"Yes. It expresses the complicated…simply. And," he said softly, looking searchingly into my eyes, "I can tell that it's…*you*."

SCENE 4

A Jam Shop:

Two women, one young and exuberant and one much older and thoughtful, stand closely together and look ahead. They are observing the discussion between two men. One is young and strikingly handsome with raven black hair and

deep brown eyes. He is facing a tall man with light-colored hair and a thin mustache, considerably older but still young. The latter throws a stack of papers onto the counter in evident frustration.

Monet [angrily]: Where are the brackets?! This is a *play*, not a novel! In a play, you have a script! In a script, you have brackets! Brackets! Do you see any brackets? [points to paper] You don't say "Colorless chandeliers attached to *blah blah blah*"! You say, [Enter Chandelier]!

Morena [mutters]: Dios mío…es peor de lo que pensaba. *(Translation: My God…it's worse than I thought.)*

Antonio [confidently]: I will write as I am inspired to write! The story did not want to be a play.

Monet [imitates]: "The story!" "The story!" He's a madman!

Elise [smiles dreamily]: He's an *artist*. [fans herself]

[**Monet** ignores **Elise** and picks up the papers again for further inspection.]

Monet: And his name is not Antonio…it's Amadeus!

Antonio: His name is Antonio! He told me so!

Monet: Who? The little voices inside your head?!
[circles finger around ear to indicate insanity]

Elise: He's an artist of great *vision*.

[**Monet** begins to move angrily towards **Antonio** as if to attack him. **Morena** steps forward quickly to stand between them, handing them each a jar of jam.]

Morena: Taste the most recent varieties of fruit jams! The very popular Dragon Fruit and, my personal favorite, Goji.

[**Antonio** and **Monet** simultaneously slam the jam jars on the counter in response.]

Elise [comfortingly, to **Morena**]: You tried.

Monet [angrily]: The Owner will hear of this!

Elise, Antonio, and Morena [simultaneously, in horror]: No!

[Enter **Fred** with pet parrot. He is wearing, as usual, his famous old, battered straw hat in the conical shape typical of Japanese design. **Fred** begins to sniff a nearby unlabeled jam jar. **Morena** approaches to serve. **Antonio** and **Monet**, unaware of the appearance of a customer, continue arguing; **Elise** looks on in concern.]

Morena [to **Fred**]: The usual, sir?

[**Fred** nods, becomes aware of argument, and silently observes.]

Morena: The usual amount?

Fred's Parrot [squawks]: The usual amount, the usual amount!

[**Morena** takes the parrot's answer as a "yes."]

Morena: One moment, sir.

[EXIT **Morena** to storage room. The audience once again is able to make out the words of the argument between **Monet** and **Antonio**.]

Monet: A blue door?! He goes in a *transparent blue door*?! How quaint! And what do you suppose we can use to show this Fountain of Transparent Youth?

Elise [excitedly, quickly]: We could use blue tissue paper!

Monet [exasperated]: BLUE TISSUE PAPER?!
BLUE TISSUE PAPER?! Of course! Why
don't we add some water from your
goldfish tank, too?! *These* are the minds that
I have to work with! [wrings hands in
despair] This is supposed to be
sophistication, not your high school drama
class! [puts hand on head]

[**Fred** continues to watch, his lips curled in
amusement. **Morena** returns with two large buckets
full of Duku jam. The argument between **Monet**
and **Antonio** now becomes inaudible to the
audience. **Elise** attempts to keep the two from
fighting.]

Morena [to **Fred**]: Planning a party, Mr. Stone?

Fred [flatly, still watching **Monet** and **Antonio**]:
Life's a party.

Morena [cautiously]: Perhaps you're having some
of your old sailor friends over? Or is the
jam for your parrot? [pauses] You wish
to…decorate your hat?

[**Fred** turns back to **Morena** with an impenetrable
gaze. **Morena** sighs with her usual acceptance of
the famous jam shop mystery.]

Morena [accepting]: And…I will ring the jam up for

you, sir.

[Argument becomes audible to the audience once again. **Elise** is standing between the two men as a "STOP" sign.]

Monet [to **Antonio**, glares]: Look what you've done…you've driven me to jam! [snatches unnamed jam jar]

[EXIT **Monet**]

Fred's parrot: Driven me to jam. [squawks] Driven me to jam.

Morena: 50 pounds of Duku jam, sir. [hands **Fred** the two buckets]

[**Antonio** and **Elise** become aware of the presence of **Fred** and their usual curiosity begins to develop.]

Elise [smiles]: Hi, Fred!

Antonio [shakes hand]: Mr. Stone, a pleasure as always! [glances at jam buckets; says casually] Duku jam again today?

[**Fred** does not respond. **Monet** re-enters, the jam jar still in one hand, but unopened.]

Monet: You're right…his name is Antonio.

[**Elise** and **Morena** breathe a sigh of relief.]

Antonio [quickly]: But I see the Amadeus.

Morena: Perhaps just a bit too bold…

Elise [finishes]: …for an uncertain character.

Monet [nods]: Yes, that's it.

[The four continue to discuss the story, but now at a more reasonable volume. **Fred** and **parrot** make way towards door. **Fred** stops just before reaching the door and looks back with a smile. EXIT.]

[EXIT ALL.]

Chapter Twelve

Tibi

"I don't even know why I'm taking this stupid class."

Chelsey and I sat, reclined, on the light brown sofas in my living room, our Spanish books open in our laps.

"You have a B+ in the class, Chelsey. You're doing very well," I said encouragingly.

"Yeah, I know. But I couldn't care less about Spanish."

Chelsey stood up, brushing strands of hair from her eyes. Her face was marked with clear distaste.

"Maybe you just need to learn more about the cultures behind the language," I suggested. "They're really…beautiful."

"No, I don't think so," she responded. "I'm just not into it."

"Okay," I nodded, accepting, but not really understanding. It was, after all, a passion of mine.

Her blonde hair rippled about her shoulders as she turned swiftly to examine a piece of art on the mantel, a sculpture of the Virgin Mary and a babe in swaddling clothes.

"Why don't we take a snack break?" I suggested. "We've been practicing irregular verb conjugations for over an hour now."

"Sure!" Chelsey turned from the mantel to face me. "I'm getting hungry!"

"Yes," I said, closing my Spanish book, "I am quite famished myself."

She walked lightly behind me as I moved towards the kitchen.

I opened the freezer door and pulled out a box of Goji fruit bars. "These are really good. I just had one last night."

"Goji?" Chelsey's light blue eyes scrunched together as I handed her the popsicle.

"It may not be for everyone, though. If you don't like it, I can get you something else," I responded amiably, sitting down at the kitchen table. Chelsey followed suit, pulling out the chair directly across from me.

We unwrapped our popsicles, and sat there in silence. My brain had probably been on Study Mode for too long. I couldn't think of anything to say.

Chelsey broke the silence, leaning eagerly towards me, "Oh my gosh! I totally forgot to tell you something!"

"Yeah?" I smiled, taking my first taste of the juicy popsicle.

"There is this new sitcom called *So You*...and oh my gosh...the guy there is like...wow! *So* cute!"

"Nice!"

"He's almost as cute as Sean Smith!"

"Sean Smith?"

"You don't know who Sean Smith is?"

I shrugged awkwardly, "I don't keep up to date on a lot of stuff. Is he an actor?"

"He's a singer! A really cute one, too."

"Nice!"

"He was on *The Tonight Show* last night!"

"Oh. I actually have never watched that show."

"You've *never* seen *The Tonight Show*?"

"Not yet."

"Oh, and there's this really hot guy that I saw at Vons yesterday. Too bad I didn't get his number. He was a-ma-zing!"

"Did you guys have a fun conversation?"

"He looked at me and smiled and I looked back at him and smiled."

"Aww, I love those wordless moments! Makes me think of Shakespeare."

"Oh, Rebecca! It wasn't like that at all. We were totally checking each other out."

"Oh," I laughed quietly, staring at my popsicle.

"But I didn't get his number. Totally lame. Oh

well…he wasn't that cute anyway."

There was a pause in the conversation.

I looked up at Chelsey and smiled. "So, did you have a nice weekend?"

"Yeah, it was cool."

"What did you do?"

"Hung out, went shopping, did homework, the usual."

"Nice. How's that psych paper going?"

"Good. Now *that* subject I like."

"We picked a great major!"

"Yeah."

"My weekend was fairly routine, too. But it was nice. Got some writing done on this story I'm working on."

"Oh…it's cute that you like that sort of thing. Oh my gosh…speaking of cute, I found the cutest shirt yesterday! It's totally the latest! You'll have to see it."

"I'm sure it's great!"

"Thanks. I also picked up some new hair dye. Have you ever thought of dying your hair?"

"Not really, actually."

"I think you'd look cute as a blonde!"

"Thanks! I don't know, though. It's not really…me."

"Oh, are you sure?"

"Yeah. Besides, I, um, tried on a blonde wig once and the results were ghastly."

"Have you ever straightened your hair?"

"No."

"You should."

Chapter Thirteen

Se

Thus, catharsis may be a pivotal breakthrough for such conditions as depression and posttraumatic stress disorder.

Stress. The perfect medicine for stress is the end of homework. Easter vacation couldn't come soon enough, I thought, as my mind took a break from my psychology paper.

I converted the one week allotted for freedom to one year, bathing in the possibilities of fun. I would have to let Adri know that we would be going to Baskin-Robbins, our old childhood haunt, at least twice a week during this momentous year.

Adri. Friends. A thought crossed my mind.

So, basically, Peter and I were hard-core kindred spirits and, other than our cyber communications, we had never hung out outside of church. In fact, we hadn't exactly had any 'writing sessions' for our story, in which we could just sit down and write together. And, dude, I told myself, what is *up* with that?

"Mom!" I bounded across the house, my flip-flops dancing gleefully on the tile floor.

Mom looked up from some papers that she was examining at the kitchen table.

"Rebecca," she said dryly, "I'm correcting French tests, you are loud, and I lost track of my counting."

"Sorry, Mom," I said quickly. "I have a proposal!"

"Proposal denied."

"Just listen for a sec, por favor," I replied earnestly. "So, you know my friend Peter from church? The dude who's working on that Canadian holiday thing?"

"Yes, I suppose."

"Well, I think that it would be fun to have him over!"

"Oh?"

"Yes, in fact, Friday afternoon is super ideal."

"Fascinating. Any reason in particular that," Mom bit her lip as a smile began to form, a glint of humor appearing in her eyes, "some 'random dude' should 'hang out' here, especially when the house is a mess?"

"But, Mom...he won't care about the mess! And he's not 'some random dude'!"

"But he's a *random* dude to me. And, regardless, he's a *dude*."

"Mom, he's an usher at *church*, he's organizing a

special event about *God*, and he's writing a story with me about a *jam shop*. Does he *sound* like a *psycho*?!"

Mom raised an eyebrow. "Jam shop?"

"Yes, specializing in Duku jam, to be precise."

Mom stared at me for a one, long moment before snapping back to her tests.

"Minus…un, deux, trois—"

"There are other kinds of jam, too. Apricot…plum…you like plum!"

"Quatre, cinq…"

I tried a different approach.

"Mom, Alexander will be home on Friday to 'slay the dragon', if necessary!"

"Clean the house. Trois, quatre—"

"*Thank you*, Mom!" I threw my arms around her neck and gave her a kiss.

"*Un*, deux, trois…"

"Peter, look out!"

The trash can slipped from my hands, rolling down the driveway and into the street, just as a visitor for 226 Snapdragon Lane arrived.

Peter put out his foot, halting its mad dash in his direction.

"Potential collision avoided!" I jumped from the driveway and ran to where he stood next to a white Honda Accord. "Excellent work!"

"So, being your friend is a safety hazard?" Peter looked up and grinned.

"Pretty much," I laughed. "That's what you get for being friends with a klutz."

"At least, being a klutz myself, I am somewhat sympathetic." Peter bent down and took hold of the bin.

He was wearing dark blue jeans and a white T-shirt with the words "Alberta Youth" spelled out in black over the material. I realized that this was the first time that I had seen him in attire that was not formal.

I led the way to the collection of trash cans at the front of the house. "Thanks for coming."

"No, thank *you*," he flashed that grin of his. "I've been wondering what the lair of a poetry-inclined psychologist looks like."

"Ha, ha…very funny."

Peter put down the trash can and we headed for the front door.

I fumbled in my purse for my keys. My mom wasn't the only one in the family with the entire family history in her purse.

Peter stood, smiling. I glared at him as I inserted the key into its lock.

"Hey, I have that Asics key chain. Got it in May of '98."

"Thank you, Mr. Precise."

Mom was in the living room, scurrying back and forth rapidly in an attempt to complete some last minute cleaning.

I smiled. "Mom, Peter won't care if the house is a mess. But it looks perfect."

Mom looked up from the stack of papers in her

hand. She raised an eyebrow and began to say something, and then noticed Peter. She came forward with a smile.

"You must be Peter!"

"Yes, Mrs. Veritas. What a pleasure to finally meet you!"

They shook hands with a formality that made me smile, too. But then I noticed an unfortunate item in my mom's left hand, and groaned.

"Mom, why must you pollute the air with that horrendous smell?!"

"Peanut butter is a gift from God," Mom said matter-of-factly, her eyes twinkling.

"More likely an experiment gone wrong," I muttered. "Besides, He made *peanuts*. Humans are the ones who proceeded to desecrate His Creation by turning it into a gooey mess."

"Peter?" Mom turned towards Peter with a look of innocence that instantly made me groan.

"Yes, Mrs. Veritas?"

"Do you like peanut butter?"

"Certainly."

Mom turned back to me, a look of triumph evident in her eyes. "I like him." With a smile and assertion that If-you-would-like-anything-to-eat-or-drink-please-let-me-know-and-so-nice-to-meet-you, Mom vanished from the room. I realized that the stack of papers in her hand were filled with some unknown code. But I did recognize the word "Bonjour!"

I snorted. *More French tests.*

"Certainly?" I protested, finally turning to Peter.

"Traitor!"

"What? Peanut butter's good for you."

"I don't care if you're the biggest health freak! That's no excuse for killing yourself. Death...by smell!" I proclaimed dramatically.

"Death by smell?"

I put my hands on my hips. "Remember how Gus from *Avonlea* worked on a pig farm when the cannery was closed for the season?"

"I do recall something of the like, yes."

I suppressed a mischievous grin. "Well..."

"Yes?"

"My mom's peanut butter smells like Gus at the cannery and my brother's favorite variety is reminiscent of Gus after he slept amongst the pigs."

Dead silence.

"I've never had the opportunity to smell either, but I'll take your word for it," Peter finally said, pursing his lips in an attempt to contain himself.

I was, once again, filled with the desire to simultaneously glare at Peter and burst into laughter. But both impulses faded as I heard a faint rustling from behind me. I turned and caught sight of our tortoise, who was rebelliously climbing atop a slight inclination on the bottom of the backyard door.

*Psycho Mood initiating...**now**.*

"Come, there is someone I'd like you to meet," I grinned with abandon.

Peter had only time for the beginnings of a barely-contained chuckle before I dragged him across the room, closing the sliding glass door behind us with a slam.

Marie Antoinette, our pet tortoise, was now making her rounds near the sliding glass door on the opposite end.

Who said that tortoises were slow?

"C'mon!" I grabbed Peter's hand again, pulling him across the yard of twinkling yellow flowers.

At that moment, I realized that I was probably close to entering The Cowboy Zone. The name was coined one day when I was really tired. I had called Adri on the phone and started talking in what she later referred to as "a very bad cowboy accent." I wasn't particularly sleep-deprived today, but I could tell where I was headed.

"Say 'hi' to Marie Antoinette, Peter."

The tortoise paused luxuriously, a movie star sunbathing.

"Hi, Marie Antoinette. Please tell me that you don't feed your tortoise much cake."

I laughed. "We try to avoid it."

Peter smiled, stooping down to gain a clearer view of the tortoise. He examined her curiously.

"You look like you've never seen a desert tortoise."

"Not in close proximity. Canada isn't exactly known for its *desert* turtles."

"Tortoises," I corrected with a grin.

"Ah, yes…tortoises," he returned the grin. "See, I'm *already* showing my ignorance."

"No worries. Probably half of the U.S. population doesn't know the difference," I laughed.

"You can feed her later," I promised with a smile as

I observed Peter peering at Marie Antoinette like someone who had forgotten to wear his glasses. He followed me to the nearby picnic table. We sat there for a few moments in silence, taking in the scene. A blue jay sang its song in the distance as the trees danced lightly in the wind. It was perfect.

"Hey, is your brother a redhead?"

I looked up. Alexander was slowly washing his hands at the kitchen sink, examining the window rather closely every few seconds.

I half-groaned, half-laughed, and walked over to the windowsill. With a crooked smile, I widened my eyes and closed the outdoor blinds as Alexander's mouth simultaneously widened in protest, only to open them once again.

"He's convinced that you're a psycho," I explained, as I reached the bench. "He has the list narrowed down to either a double agent or a serial killer."

"He's right."

I raised an eyebrow.

He laughed. "Not that I'm a psycho. At least, not a psycho in a bad way. But there are a lot of psychos out there and you have to be careful."

"Oh, I am. Some people probably think that I'm too cautious. I say, 'Better safe than sorry.' But I trust my friends and…that includes you," I concluded with a smile, as I played with the zipper of my jacket.

"Thank you for your trust," Peter said quietly. "It means a lot to me."

I looked up just in time to see a dark shadow creep across Peter's face. I suddenly realized why I had been so quick to interject my point. It hadn't been a point about *me*. Something in Peter's voice had made me want to finish up with the topic as quickly as possible.

That, and a moment of hyper bliss promised to approach. But, as half of an idea formed in the recesses of my mind, Peter spoke first.

"Oh, I almost forgot." Peter dug his hand into his pocket. "I think you'll find this to be useful. Besides, for some reason, it reminded me of you."

He looked up, his eyes resting on my shirt, and laughed. "And I didn't even know anything about your weekday wardrobe."

It was a pen of a pink floral design. *Like my shirt.*

I lightly traced the intricate design with a single finger. "Thank you so much! It's very pretty. And I will definitely put it to good use!"

Peter smiled. "No problem."

"But I don't have anything to give you!"

"You welcomed me into your home," Peter said simply.

"Well, yeah, but still—" my words ended as I caught sight of the swing set and The Idea became whole.

"I have an idea!" I exclaimed.

Peter cleared his throat. "The last time you said that, we were whisked away on an exciting adventure in the world of strange ex-sailors with parrots and a borderline obsession with Duku jam. I'm not sure if I'm up for another challenge *quite* yet."

I laughed. "It's nothing like that, though we should definitely work on *Intermission* today."

Peter nodded in agreement. "Certainly."

"I was thinking more along the lines of something crazily and awesomely *childish*."

Peter shrugged. "You know my major. In other words, sure."

"Great. Let's go on the swings."

"Sounds good," Peter chuckled. "Do you have a swing set or are we taking a field trip to the local park?"

"As a matter of fact, we do." I gestured towards the nearby tree from which hung two wooden swings.

"Dad put them up for Alex and me when we were little," I explained as we walked towards the sycamore tree. "We convinced him to keep them up for stress relief during finals week."

"Nice."

I reached out a hand, taking hold of the left cord of rope, and slid into the seat. Peter sat down on the swing next to me.

"Is this stable?" He looked at the tree, raising an eyebrow.

His eyes laughed merrily, yet his body seemed stiff.

"You don't know my dad. He would never let us use it if it weren't one hundred percent safe."

Peter nodded, relaxing his tight grip on the cords of rope.

"So, you know how I'm kind of in an immature mood?"

Peter grinned. "Yeah, I gathered as much right around when you dragged me across your house into the backyard. But, hey, it's not immaturity, just expressing your inner child, which is a healthy activity to partake in every once in a while."

"Am I not the psychologist?" I protested, a smile working its way across my face.

Peter smiled and, as if in response to my rhetorical question, lifted his feet off of the ground. I immediately followed suit, quickly gaining in speed.

Faster and faster.

"*I* like to swing with my eyes closed," I announced with all the pride of a ten-year-old school girl.

"Thanks for the memo. Hey, aren't you in Mrs. Wilder's third grade class?"

"No, I'm in *fifth* grade, my little *first* grade friend."

"I was in first grade 26 times 5 minus 3 times 9 divided by 2 years ago."

I laughed. "Did you even do the math for that?"

"Yes."

I snorted. "And you're still going by that answer?"

"Absolutely."

"I bet I can go higher than you can!" I challenged, raising the pitch of my voice several octaves.

"Really, Rebecca, haven't you had enough trauma for one day? Aren't you afraid of devolving permanently to a less mature mental state? Now, let me see...what is the current psychological jargon for such an occurrence?"

"Regression," I said slowly, emphasizing each word as if I were really speaking with a first grader. "And don't worry about me. My *identity* is too strong as to result in such a *psychological dilemma*."

Peter grinned and began to swing more rapidly.

"Guess I'm the better swinger."

"Never!" I shouted with abandon, gleefully moving forward on my majestic steed. "To the top of the tallest tree!"

"You're on!"

"Bet you can't do that with your eyes closed!"

"Oh yeah?"

We sped rapidly back and forth, the exciting rush of unknown territory filling our lungs.

Unknown.

"Wait…who's winning?"

We both opened our eyes sheepishly.

"It was your idea to ride blind. But, anyway, I'm winning. Just like I did on January 4, 1996 at 2:34 PM to a Mr. Timothy Bonwagon."

"Mr. Precise yet again?"

"Yep."

"I'm Italian, so I automatically win."

"Hmm, I know that Italians are known for many great achievements, but I wasn't aware that swing races were among them."

"We're the best at everything."

"Canadians can swing in their sleep."

"Is that why you're losing right now? Because you're *asleep*?"

"I'm just observing that blue jay's flight so that I might imitate it and descend victorious."

"If you try to distract me, you'll automatically lose."

"Me, try to distract you? Besides, I *am* winning."

"Not so!"

"Yes, I am!"

"No, *I* am!"

And, with laughter and lunacy, we flew high above the world.

SCENE 7

A Local Park:

[ENTER **Elise** and **Antonio**]

Elise [enthusiastically]: I really love your new watch!

Antonio [looks ahead searchingly]: I've had it for the past ten years.

Elise [quickly]: It's...timeless!

[**Antonio** ignores **Elise** and continues to survey his surroundings.]

Elise [clears throat]: Do you like ice cream?

Antonio [absentmindedly]: Yes.

Elise [with a mixture of eagerness and uncertainty]:
Me, too! You know, since *you* like ice cream
and *I* like ice cream, maybe we should—

[ENTER **Monet**]

Antonio [triumphantly]: *There* he is! Now I can
demonstrate my superiority once and for
all!

[**Antonio** marches in the direction of **Monet**'s path.
Elise looks on and sighs.]

Elise [comfortingly]: He loves me.

[EXIT **Elise**]

Monet: Are you ready?

Antonio: Ready to send you to The Lost Archives
of Alcatraz!

Monet [laughs]: He is so confident! *Fool.*

[**Antonio** and **Monet** walk briskly to the nearest
table, which is under a great Redwood tree. They sit
down and instantaneously take out a deck of cards
each.]

Monet: Ha! Like I'd trust the cards of a *malheureux*
like you!

Antonio: I am not sure what you called me, but you will pay dearly for it, *disgraziato*!

[ENTER **Morena** with jam pie.]

Morena: Would you two gentlemen care for some dessert?

Antonio [angrily points to **Monet**]: He will be our dessert when I am finished with him!

Morena [calmly]: So, what's the game today?

Antonio and Monet [simultaneously]: Arm wrestling! [glare at each other]

Morena: Ah, the usual. Well, if you change your mind, the Wolfberry jam pie will be in the kitchen. I'll be working on my scene of "Muse."

Antonio [corrects]: "Midnight Moonlight: The Story." Or, simply, "The Story."

Monet [growls]: It is called MUSE!

[**Antonio** and **Monet** quickly get up and move towards each other.]

Morena [commands]: ¡Siéntense!

[**Monet** and **Antonio** reluctantly obey, sitting down abruptly with a sniff.]

Antonio: We will combine the two decks. Compromise.

Monet [growls]: Fine! Parlay.

[EXIT **Morena**. ENTER **Elise**. **Elise** watches as **Antonio** and **Monet** throw down the cards of their respective decks onto the center of the table and move them around with broad circular motions.]

Elise [pauses]: Interesting shuffling technique.

Antonio [throws a few cards in the air]: At last we have finished. The Crazy 8s game may now commence.

Monet: Challenge accepted.

Elise [interjects]: Uh, don't you guys have to deal out the cards?

Antonio and Monet [glare at Elise; simultaneously]: I know that!

[They deal out eight cards each. The remaining cards are put in a pile at the center of the table.]

Monet: You draw first, muskrat.

Antonio [draws card with exaggerated elegance]:
Queen of Hearts.

Elise [smiles at **Antonio**]: My favorite card.

[**Monet** puts down the Queen of Spades. **Antonio** examines it thoroughly.]

Antonio: Acceptable. [puts down a five of spades]

Elise [cheers]: Go, Antonio! Go, Antonio!

[**Monet** glares at **Elise**.]

[The game continues in this manner for some time.]

Antonio: Ah, an 8. I choose.

Monet [growls]: Hurry up, prince.

Antonio [grins]: I choose…diamonds!

Monet [furiously]: You maligned fur ball! You
knew that I had to draw for diamonds last
time.

Antonio [sighs happily]: Rules are rules.

[**Monet** collects ten cards before finally getting an

ace of diamonds.]

Monet [throws card down on stack]: There!

Antonio [sighs]: Alas, this party must come to an end. [puts down final card, which is another "8," thereby winning the game]

Monet [quickly stands up]: You cheated, you, you... [begins to throw cards at him] misérable!

Antonio [ducks]: I played honorably! It is you that plays poorly!

Monet [continues the card attack]: Think I wouldn't notice that you got all the 8s? Hmmm?! You sabotaged this game!

Antonio [takes up his own cards and begins to throw them at **Monet** in rapid succession]: I did not!

[The battle continues steadily. **Monet** and **Antonio** are about to deplete their remaining ammunition when a shriek is heard in the vicinity. Both turn around to find **Elise** running away.]

Antonio: If I knew it were that easy, I'd throw cards more often.

Monet: She's not running away from you, fool!
[points wildly at nearby tree]

[A swarm of bees march purposely towards the two. **Monet** and **Antonio** look at each other for a moment with terrified expressions and then begin to run after **Elise**, screaming.]

[ENTER **Morena**. She looks back and forth between the flight of her friends and the flight of the bees and stifles a laugh.]

Morena [shakes head]: "En boca cerrada, no entran moscas." Or, in this case, *abejas. (Proverb: "In a closed mouth, no flies will enter." Or, in this case, bees.)*

[**Morena** waits until the bees depart and then begins to follow her friends at a leisurely pace. She finds them, finally halted in a small field and breathing heavily. She begins to make out their conversation.]

Elise [moans]: I hate bees!

Monet [angrily, to **Antonio**]: You, it was you! You called the bees!

Antonio [looks at **Elise**, pointing to **Monet**]: He is mad! Lost his mind! Gone insane! Calling the bees, indeed! What do you think I am...a dandelion?!

Monet: It's still your fault! You distracted me! I could have been stung!

Antonio: *I* could have been stung!

Elise [sighs]: My poor Antonio! My hero! You saved me!

Monet: Saved you?! He didn't see the bees until you screamed!

Antonio [to **Monet**]: And you ran, screaming, like a scared little GIRL!

Monet [shouts]: I screamed?! YOU screamed!

Morena [approaching]: You both screamed, no one saved Elise, and all of you could have been stung. Now, either quit arguing or quit eating The Jam Shop's jam for the rest of your lives! [looks at **Monet**] And that includes you, Monet! Not one more spoonful of Vegetable Brains jam will you have!

[Nearly inaudible grumbling from **Monet** and **Antonio** is heard, but silence ensues quickly.]

Morena [authoritatively, looks at **Monet**]: Speaking

of which, Monet, I found a jar of apricot jam this morning that was not its natural color.

[**Monet** shifts feet nervously.]

Morena [continues]: In fact, there was something in that same jar—a *purple* something—that greatly resembled plum jam. Have you been mixing jams again lately, Monet?

Monet [stammers]: Uhhh, of course not! It is forbidden in the jam shop!

Antonio [points at **Monet** victoriously]: He did it! I saw him!

[**Monet** glares at **Antonio** and moves towards him.]

Elise [looks ahead quickly and points]: Look, swings!

Monet [rolls eyes]: What are we, ten-year-olds?

[**Elise** starts to run to the swings excitedly. **Morena** and **Antonio** glance at each other, a smile of youthfulness filling their eyes before they quickly follow suit. **Monet** remains for a moment and, then, with some grumbling, runs after them. They all grab a swing and begin to fly high to the sky. Laughter is heard…laughter of four, united as one.]

"Swings, jam, and Crazy 8s," I said, settling down into the large spinning chair in front of the computer that I called my throne. "But is all of this random insanity connected by a theme?" I mused.

"Of course not," Peter grinned, carefully unwrapping a Goji fruit bar. "Isn't that the point?"

"Yes…I mean, no!"

"The madness is the logic that connects everything…because…"

"…the madness is important," I finished.

Peter nodded thoughtfully, eating his popsicle. "Yes."

"So," I began slowly, "maybe what is really important is not the fact that they're writing a play or maintaining a jam shop, but…the little things in between."

"The space between the notes," Peter quoted softly.

And then the doorbell rang.

How cliché.

"We're almost done with this scene," I arose with a grunt.

"Intermission?" Peter raised an eyebrow.

"Ha, ha." I rolled my eyes and opened the door.

It was Adriana.

"The Pepper Pirate!" she sputtered, stepping inside in one long, exasperated leap.

"The Pepper…what?"

"The Pepper Pirate!" Adriana repeated impatiently,

rapidly pacing back and forth across the small expanse of the entryway. "Here I am, watching a *serious* superhero adventure—like one from the good old days of comic strips—well, up until *now*—I mean, *dude*, it has The Terrible Tarantula and The Horned Toad...how *epic* is that?!?—and then they bring in The Pepper Pirate and ruin everything! What is *wrong* with people today?! Has the world gone completely *ballistic*?! Has the galaxy suddenly *exploded* into a thousand scattered pieces of Pez dispensers? Is the universe—"

It was at this moment in a characteristic Adriana ranting rampage that she noticed a hitherto unaccustomed presence in my living room. She stopped short, cocking her head in confusion and blinking. She then proceeded to peer scientifically at Peter and, slowly, recognition dawned upon her.

"You're the usher dude, aren't you?"

Thank you, Adriana.

I laughed awkwardly and gave her a hug. She drew back sharply in puzzlement. "But, Rebecca, what is the usher dude doing in *your* house?"

"¿Cómo *estás*, Adriana?" I said through my teeth, fixing upon her an intense glare.

"Once again, she speaks in another language when things get awkward," Adriana said cheerfully, jumping off the step to approach Peter.

I eyed a rather large pillow on the nearest sofa, but thought better of it.

Peter stood up, instantly shaking Adri's hand. *Eternally tall and polite. For those who didn't know better, that is.* "Pleased to meet you. I'm Peter Asturian. Or," he flashed one of his characteristic half-amused-but-too-polite-to-completely-show-it grins. "Usher Dude, if you'd prefer."

"Adriana Hanson," my dark-haired friend responded cordially. "And, duly noted."

Good. She was behaving herself now. Adriana could be one of the most well-mannered people you knew, but, when she got hyped up, you never knew what might happen.

Kind of like me, I admitted with a smile, finally stepping down to join my two friends.

"By the way, you're right," Peter turned back to Adriana after briefly noting my approach with a smile, "The Pepper Pirate *was* a ghastly addition to what otherwise might have easily been considered the best comic strip story of the century."

Adriana stared at Peter, wide-eyed, turned towards me, her eyes beaming with excitement, and then turned back to Peter again.

I knew exactly what she was thinking. It was not often that even I, considered eccentric by many, could make heads or tails of Adriana's superhero rants. Despite our numerous inside jokes that were unintelligible to the outside world, this special brand of Adriana Rants remained incomprehensible to even me. But Peter had not only followed her train of thought, but actually knew what she was talking about. I watched as respect, the deepest sort with which she favored few, washed over Adriana's face, and a smile swept across my own. Two people, one who had been my best friend for most of my life and another, a new friend who had quickly gained significance, were, from all indications, about to become good friends. There was something special about that…something special about watching your friends become friends with each other…like a story arc reaching its full potential. Something almost magical despite its subtlety… perhaps *because* of that subtlety. *The "little" things…*

Especially when potential for a trio was in the picture. There was always something special about a trio.

But, in spite of all of this, I could not help but be amused by it all. Peter had never struck me as the comic strip type.

Everyone really is full of surprises, surprises that come out when you least expect them…some good, some bad, some a bit of both. I thought.

As cliché as that sounded.

As cliché as truth can sound.

As real as truth can be.

And, with these thoughts and assorted others, I watched my two friends effervescently chatting — interjecting a point or two every once in a while (*"Why is The Terrible Turnip more dignified than The Pepper Pirate?" I queried, to which I received two impassive scowls and decided to say nothing further on the subject.*) — but, mostly, taking a step back, quietly observing, smiling, and thinking.

Between The Cackling Cowboy and The Ferocious Flying Ferris Wheel, Adriana and Peter barely noticed.

Chapter Fourteen

Cor

It was the fourth Sunday of Lent.

Happy belated birthday. You're an awesome person, amiga. :D

Peter had, much to my surprise, sent me an e-card.

I shook my head and automatically smiled. An involuntary giggle instantly escaped. I heard my brother mutter, "Weirdo," from the next room, but I barely noticed. For some reason, something so…*ridiculous*…but wonderfully anomalous made me feel like I was floating on a cloud of absolute mirth and happiness. It was probably what I would have thought laughing gas was like, had I not experienced it first-hand prior to a wisdom teeth extraction. At the time, I had felt like my breath was being sucked out of me.

But, now, in this moment, I guess my breath was 'sucked out' of me in a different—and certainly much more pleasant—way.

I gleefully pressed the "Print" icon, unable to stop smiling.

Thank God it was Sunday.

As much as I loved Mass, I was somewhat distracted. I saw him at the Presentation of the Gifts, basket in hand. As our eyes met, he grinned, his lips pressed closely together as if to stifle a laugh. I placed my envelope in the basket with more firmness than necessary and looked up at him, raising an eyebrow. He lifted an eyebrow in return, as if to condemn unseemly behavior. Yet I knew from his dancing eyes that we were on the same page.

At the end of Mass, I marched to the front of the usher's closet where he stood, deep in conversation with Cedric, and thrust the printed copy of the e-card into his surprised hands. The old man eyed us both with his usual amusement before retreating with a wave of farewell. He stepped into the usher's closet, beginning to organize stacks of paper as if he had entered the church with no other intention.

"My birthday was in January, Mr. Asturian." I pressed "Replay" on the eyebrow gesture.

"Ah, yes," he said, his lips again pressed intentionally together. "Adriana informed me of that fact, so I made haste to congratulate you. I was already quite late, you see," he added matter-of-factly.

"So, are you going to send me a Christmas card, too?" I protested, hands on my hips.

"Well, now that you mention it…"

His grin had completely won me over, and I could no longer pull off my façade. We both burst out laughing. When our laughter finally ceased, I looked up at him and shook my head.

"You are so…" I sputtered in an inability to find the words or prevent the ridiculously-irrepressible grin from spreading across my face, "are so…so…*weird*," I finally found the word.

"Why, thank you. I take that as a compliment."

"Hey, you're changing the code," I protested with a smile.

"Author's privilege."

I had truly met a kindred spirit.

I was blessed.

It was the Intermission.

I pushed down the lever of the paper towel dispenser.

Adriana and I had taken the opportunity provided by the break in the play to take a trip to the restroom.

The play. It was an adaptation of *My Fair Lady*, my favorite musical, playing for the entire week at my college. It might have also been Adriana's favorite musical since she despised all musicals equally. With much grumbling, she had assented to its viewing in the name of Homework. To me, it sounded like the least bizarre activity that her major of Theater Arts required.

Chelsey was occupied with visiting family, so I alone held the responsibility of accompanying Adriana on this perilous journey.

And perilous, it was indeed. Adriana seemed to be suffering from several ancient diseases throughout the first two acts of the play.

"Rebecca?"

I immediately turned with concern at the question in her voice.

Her brow was creased slightly in uncertainty as she shifted her feet awkwardly.

"Rebecca," she said slowly, "I've been a bit at odds with Chelsey lately."

Chapter Fifteen

Meum

I waited, my face tightening.

"…especially after she told me not to invite you to our next Golden Spoon outing."

My head whirled as some unseen motion entered my chest with piercing reality. I took a deep breath.

"Did she mention why?"

Adriana hesitated. "I don't think it's really necessary for you to hear that."

"Just say it, please."

"Please promise me that this will stay between us…?

"Of course."

"Rebecca, are you sure that you…want—"

"Yes."

"Okay." Adriana cleared her throat and began to stare intently at her feet. I felt a sudden desire to comfort her, even though it was I who…

Adriana looked up, her eyebrows scrunched closely together. I left my thoughts and simply nodded.

"She said that you were," she paused, "weird…and that…it embarrassed her to be around you."

"Oh."

"Which makes me wonder why *I* wasn't kicked out of the club, being the bigger oddball in the group," she made an attempt at a laugh.

I heard the cheerful sound of chimes beckoning the audience to their seats. The intermission had ended.

"C'mon," I grabbed Adriana's hand and pulled her through the door.

I didn't see the rest of the play. *I couldn't.* I didn't see yesterday, or even the latest moments in time.

I saw nothing.

And nothingness enveloped me.

Adriana had to pick up her younger brother from his swim meet. She offered me one last, fleeting glance as she left.

I trudged ahead.

Weird or odd…it really didn't matter which word was used, did it?

A light flickered in the distance; it emanated from the computer lab. I figured that I would check my email as I waited to be picked up by my brother.

I entered the room. I sat down at the nearest computer.

An icy coldness had attacked my chest and I could feel nothing.

I typed in my email address and password.

I waited.

And, there, in the Inbox, was a single email. It stared out at me in bold.

I clicked on it.

```
Heavenly Father, guide Rebecca as
she prepares her schedule for next
semester, and all other semesters.
Let it be filled with only as much
insanity as she wishes. In Jesus'
Name, Amen.

Your loyal servant,
Peter
```

For several moments, my eyes did not leave the computer screen.

He didn't even know. He gave this to me without knowing that I was hurting, that my feelings had exceeded far beyond the uncertainty that accompanied the planning of a semester schedule. He did something as a true friend would do. And I realized that, although I had, physically, spent less time with him than Chelsey, I was closer to him than I would have ever been to her in a thousand years. What Chelsey had done would never have even crossed his mind for an instant.

Waves of warmth began to return to my numb body. And a microscopic tear escaped my eye.

Chapter Sixteen

Totum

It was the thirtieth day of Lent.

I did not blame her.

She was immature...as everyone was in one way or another. Yet it was as if she were stuck in the high school maze of giggles, gossip, and drama. I had acknowledged this before, but, perhaps, not as consciously as I could have. Deep inside, I think that I had always known that this would serve as a barrier...a barrier that would keep me from becoming truly close to her.

We had never had, nor would we ever have, the camaraderie that I shared with Adriana and Peter.

Yet I knew that she had not done this to hurt me. And, as I gazed at the Crucifix before me, I realized that I forgave her. Truly, really, honestly.

But it still hurt. It hurt *so much*.

It was the end of Mass. I put on my sweater, fastening each button deliberately.

I had attended daily Mass on impulse. I guess I needed…peace of mind. And now I would return home in the car that I had borrowed from my dad.

"Rebecca?"

I turned, and suddenly realized that I had reached the back of the church. I must have walked there, but it had slipped from my memory.

Peter stood, a brilliant smile beginning to illuminate his countenance. It dimmed and slowly faded as Peter studied my face for one long moment.

Strange. Peter had said that he only served on Sundays.

"Rebecca, would you like to follow me outside?" he asked quietly.

I obeyed almost robotically, my body moving behind him while my mind lay dormant. When Peter stopped right in front of the church, I almost ran into him.

We leaned against the cool surface of the wall. A long silence ensued as we both studied the ground beneath our feet. I had no words and Peter offered none.

When I finally looked up, Peter was gazing quietly

ahead, seemingly deep in thought. I stared at his profile. I had never before noticed the sharpness of his chin or the narrow angle of his nose. I guess I had never had a reason to notice.

Peter was Peter, and that was all that came to surface.

"There is someone I would like you to meet," Peter finally said, breaking the silence. "Will you come?" He moved away from the wall, and waited. I pulled my sweater closer around me, and, with it, his words. I moved forward.

Peter kept the same pace that I did, even though I knew that I helplessly dragged my feet. The image of a doctor guiding an invalid grudgingly entered my mind. Yet there was a companionable silence as we trudged onward. My mind was still half vacant, but I felt safe. And, although our hands did not touch, I felt as if they did.

I soon realized that we were approaching the Adoration Chapel. It was a small, brown and white structure, surrounded by the pinks, reds, and whites of delicate roses. I followed Peter inside.

Four or five rows of wooden pews came into view. They were all vacant. In fact, as I scanned my surroundings, I realized that there seemed to be no one in the chapel at all.

I turned towards Peter in confusion. "There's no one here."

"On the contrary," he said softly, "everyone is here."

I looked beyond the pews, beyond myself, and there, on the altar, in a golden monstrance, was the

Blessed Sacrament.

Peter genuflected, making the Sign of the Cross, and entered the first set of pews. I followed.

I knelt before the altar.

There was a quiet stillness in this place, yet it was not one of unnerving discomfort, but of peace. I breathed in the air of heavenly tranquility that surrounded me.

All is calm, all is bright.

I crossed myself.

In the Name of the Father, and of the Son, and of the Holy Spirit.

I felt a prayer.

My Dear Lord, please help me. Place me in the Center of Your Perfect Will.

Adoro te devote, latens Deitas.

Bread of Life by bread concealed, speaking heart to heart.

Tibi se cor meum totum subiicit.

Let Your presence draw me in where my senses fail.

Visus, tactus, gustus in te fallitur.

This is truth enough for me.

Peto quod petivit latro paenitens.

Seeing You upon the Cross, flesh and blood, I find.

Plagas, sicut Thomas, non intueor

I see not but name You still God and Prince of Life.

O memoriale mortis Domini.

How I thirst to meet Your gaze gloriously revealed. After life's obscurity, let me wake to see. Beauty shining from Your Face for eternity.

Amen.

Chapter Seventeen

Subiicit

When I saw Chelsey the next day, a pang throbbed in my chest. She was sitting, relaxed, at a table in the hall, looking through her notebook. A lock of hair fell slightly over one eye.

She couldn't know.

She couldn't know that I knew. I had made a promise to Adriana. And, even if I hadn't, I knew that this was a promise that I would have made to myself.

But this feeling...of seeing her...of looking her straight in the face with the knowledge that was mine to bear...

"Hey, Rebecca!" Chelsey looked up from the sheets

of paper and smiled.

I smiled back.

Perhaps she saw it. I didn't know for sure.

After we walked into psychology class, placed our belongings on the floor, and were finally seated, she turned towards me, her eyebrows scrunched slightly together.

"How are you?"

I paused. "Kinda tired. I didn't get much sleep last night."

Chelsey nodded, and turned back to the doodling in her notebook.

So, she had noticed.

As I turned the key in the lock, I heard the sound of the phone ringing in the distance. I sighed, and quickly opened the door to dash across the house.

"Hello?"

"Hi, Lighthousekeeper45!"

It was our old phone code.

"Oh, hi, Dad!"

"Is Mom home?"

"Not yet. She's at the grocery store."

"Okay, can you tell her that I'm going to be a little late? I'm going to visit Monsignor McGregor.

Things...don't look too good."

I closed my eyes.

In the late evening, a key, struggling to insert itself into the lock, jangled half-heartedly at the front door. My dad entered. His shirt was the brightest of blues, but I saw only the dimmest echo of color.

Mom embraced his worn and ashen face. Taking his hand, she led him to the table.

A fog surrounded him as he pulled out a chair and sat down. He stared absentmindedly ahead.

"Monsignor isn't...well, but he sure has his old vigor."

Dad smiled in recollection, his eyes moist.

"He told me that he had always thought of me as his son, as his own flesh and blood. I'll...never forget that."

"I'll be praying for him."

"Thanks, Adri," I twisted the phone cord absentmindedly.

"You're welcome."

"So, now that we've covered *my* weekend...how's yours been?"

"Pretty chill. I had some time to relax and do nothing."

"How late did you sleep in?" I teased.

"Ha, ha. Actually, I got a lot of little things done. I just mailed a birthday card to Robby."

Adriana and her family had moved away to Colorado for two years. We talked on the phone all the time, and it seemed that Robby, her closest friend and neighbor, made his way into every conversation.

"Oh, sweet!"

"Yeah, it was nice to have a day off…to do stuff."

I laughed. "So much for doing nothing."

"Is nothing something or something nothing?"

"Inquiring minds want to know!"

"Indeed!"

"'LOL'. So, how was that movie that you saw last night?"

"Dude!"

"That good?"

"Yep. It had an explosion in the beginning and an explosion at the end, and several explosions in between."

I laughed, "Figures. Sounds like Adriana Paradise."

"Ha, ha. The plot was really good, too."

"Would I like it?"

"Probably not."

"Too many explosions?"

"And too little romance."

"Ah, gotcha!"

"Yep."

There was a slight pause in the conversation. Somehow, despite the distance, despite the absence of facial expressions that I could analyze, I knew that

Adriana wanted to say something and wasn't quite sure how. I saw the facial expressions in my mind's eye. *In my heart.*

"Dude, I'm sorry."

"For what?"

"For leaving you after the play."

She didn't need to say which play. What other play was there?

"Oh, don't even worry about it."

"But I *am* sorry. I feel like...I should have been there for you more than I was. Especially since I was the one who spit out the bad news."

"It's fine, Adri."

"No, I don't think it is."

"Dude—"

"If it hadn't been for my brother's swim meet—"

"I didn't want you to be late to pick up your brother," I said firmly. "Besides, I don't think...I would have been able to say much at the time. I wouldn't have really...felt like talking."

"But I could have been there, at least."

"Dude, you're always there for me," I said gently.

"As are you. I just wish that I could have been there for you *then*."

"In spirit, you were."

"You're just trying to be nice."

"I knew that you cared. That's what mattered."

"Is this another 'It's the thought that counts' moment?"

"Since clichés don't exist, sure."

"I'm still going by my original conclusions. I

wanted to be there."

"And that is one of the many reasons that you are my 'sister'."

"Aww, thanks."

"No problem, chica."

"Oh! Speaking of clichés and all that, I finally got around to reading that chapter you sent me."

"Of *Intermission*?"

"Yeah, yeah. Dude, you guys did a great job! I was laughing hysterically and fell out of my chair!"

"I was about to say, 'Thank you!', but now I'm more inclined to say, 'I'm sorry'!"

"Nah, all's good, mate. The floor had a lot of padding."

"If you say so, Captain Hanson."

"Long live Intermission!"

"Indeed."

Chapter Eighteen

Quia

It was the fifth Friday of Lent.

I saw a piece of folded paper drop lightly into the basket.

Not again.

I looked up, catching a glimpse of a wide grin on Peter's face before he quickly moved on to the next row.

I looked down again, barely making out the letters "c" and "a" on the piece of paper before a piercing shriek came from my right. A small boy, no more than four years of age, had evidently tripped on my purse, which lay to the right of me on the floor. Sympathy overtook me and I instantly forgot about the mysterious note as I helped the boy to his feet and wiped his eyes with a handkerchief that I kept in the incriminating purse. His mother smiled a "thank you," and I regained my seat just in time to notice the offertory basket make its way to the next row. I nearly stood up in panic, briefly imagining myself leaping across the aisle to grab the note to the chagrin of my fellow parishioners and the detriment of the small boy in my row.

I recomposed myself, sitting tall and calm.

Oh, well. I would retrieve the note — or whatever it was — after Mass.

"Rebecca dear, it's been so long!"

I turned around and smiled instantly at the sound of a familiar accent intermixed with a familiar voice. An elderly woman from Ireland that I had befriended a few years before, Constance, approached me with a warm smile.

I loved that woman like an aunt, but time was of the essence.

"Nice to see you, Constance!" I embraced my friend.

"How's school?"

"Good!"

"And life?"

"Good!"

"A special someone in your life?"

Define special.

"Oh, no...not really."

"You can't hide from Aunty Constance, dear! Is he tall? Handsome? Does he write you thoughtful notes and beautiful poetry like you deserve?"

Thoughtful notes?

"You have no idea," I smiled, as I planned a rather interesting encounter with my new friend which would require some ducking on his part.

"Well, keep him on his toes!"

Oh, believe me...I plan to!

"Of course."

Constance kissed me lightly on the cheek, giving me an affectionate squeeze before moving toward the nearest seat for her usual after-Mass prayers.

After quickly examining my surroundings like a secret agent on a mission, I marched with purpose towards the double doors that seemed to salute me as I neared.

Go, Rebecca, go!

The usher's closet was only a few feet away. I eagerly approached the door. I was pretty sure that the collection baskets were kept there.

I stopped short as a tall figure loomed in front of the door, blocking my entrance.

*Tall and **big**.*

I instantly recognized the man before me as one of the Roman guards from last year's Good Friday Passion Play.

I'm sure he was a nice guy, but, right now, he was just big, bulky, and scary. Right now he was the Roman guard.

But I was also a Roman...on a mission. I cleared my throat and stood up as tall as I could.

"Hi." My face reddened awkwardly. *So much for the mission.*

"Hi," he said in a booming voice that I somehow expected, even though the "Roman guard" was not a speaking role. "May I help you?"

"Sure," I hesitated. *How exactly would I put it?*

Roman Guard stood, waiting.

"I forgot something," I admitted, feigning an innocent laugh.

"Oh, some folks dropped off items over here in the Lost and Found," he nodded in understanding. "Follow me." Roman Guard opened the door of the usher closet, placing a big, bulky (I couldn't get those adjectives out of my head.) object against the door to keep it open.

"Thank you...so much." I eyed the shelves before me, hesitating over what to do next, as I stared at mislaid purses, assorted jackets, and the occasional Missal.

I cleared my throat again. *As if that had helped last time.*

"Um...I sorta left my belongings elsewhere."

"Right. Which is why we're looking here."

"Oh, right!"

"Would you like to check the pews first?"

"Uh, no...not really. Don't think I'd find it...there."

Roman Guard surveyed me with a puzzled expression.

Okay, I really had to say something. Roman Guard was trying to be helpful.

"First off, what's your name?" I asked lightly. Things would come out better if Roman Guard were not his name.

"Bob."

That didn't help. I bit my lip to contain my amusement. *Bob the Roman Guard.* I wasn't quite sure why I found that to be entertaining, but I did.

"Hey, I'm Rebecca!"

That didn't help either. Why did I just identify myself, accomplice to criminal activity that I was?

"Hi…Rebecca," Bob squinted, looking as if he had just encountered a stampede of raging elephants at close proximity.

"So, uh, Bob?" My statement became a question.

He nodded, nearly closing his eyes as he attempted to stand there politely.

"Well, you see," I began again, "my belongings were…dropped into one of the offertory baskets."

There. The no-fault clause in Spanish served its purpose. *Se me cayó.* It fell all on its own.

All on its own? I stifled a laugh. But what else was I supposed to say? One of your fellow ushers dropped a lovely note into the offertory basket for me? A future delinquent in Catholic history who was now MIA?

"Oh," Bob ~~the Roman Guard~~ looked relieved. He probably would still nominate me for The Weirdo of the Century™ award, but at least his task was done.

I nodded, attempting a smile. My face was still red…I just knew it. But my mission was complete.

"Well, gee, I'd love to help, but the offertory gifts were already taken down to the parish center."

*Internal face palm commences…**now**.*

I took a deep breath, attempting to hide my anguish. "I will…head over there…now. Thanks for your help."

"No problem." Roman Guard ~~Bob~~ was still standing there, watching me with a bemused expression, as I made my way towards the exit.

The parish center. That would be a long walk. Good thing that Mom had decided to visit the Adoration Chapel after Mass.

Once again, I had attended daily Mass. Perhaps I would continue to do so in honor of Lent, in addition to forty days without chocolate. Today Mom had chosen to accompany me.

And, apparently, Peter had also decided to accompany me, once again breaking his usher tradition just to torment me.

I crossed myself, closing the door lightly behind me to begin the next steps of my mission. As my hand drew apart from the door handle, I recalled an earlier day in which my best friend of twelve years had, by this very door, nearly dragged me out of the place. I shook my head with a smile.

It had been Ash Wednesday. The first day of Lent and the first day I saw Peter. And the first note I had received in this unorthodox fashion…the mysterious piece of paper revealing the word "Intermission."

Was it Peter?

I paused in my walk. *It had to be. Who else?* He was

the one who had handed me the basket, after all. The events of today surely provided all the evidence I needed to confirm the identity of the one responsible for that random happenstance.

But why? He couldn't have possibly known that it would inspire our story. He didn't even know me then. Was the scrap of paper even meant for me? Was it meant for someone else? Or no one in particular?

It's not like it had my name on it.

My hand brushed against my purse where the small, golden piece of paper still lay.

Nor would the handwriting be of any assistance because this note was type-written.

Of course.

Pure randomness?

I shook my head with a smile.

Maybe that's how they do things in Canada.

Yet, despite all the logic that seemed to indicate the named culprit of Peter, both then and now, something about it didn't seem quite right. It would be...out of character for Peter to play a joke—or whatever it was—on someone that he did not know. Despite all the contradictions within him, Peter was still the quiet sort.

Did I know him as well as I thought I did?

I absentmindedly ran my hand through my hair and, with it, my scrambled thoughts. My interest in detective work quickly expired as I noticed a foreign substance in my hair. A rather *wet*, but not altogether foreign, foreign substance.

I looked up into the sky and groaned. It was raining.

God definitely had a sense of humor.

And I did not have an umbrella.

I walked as quickly as I could while still maintaining my ability to avoid puddles and not slip and fall in the darkening brown pavement.

Typical Rebecca. Once again I had been so completely absorbed with my inner ponderings that I had failed to notice the most basic state of my surroundings.

When it rains, it pours.

In a few minutes, a light sprinkling had turned into a raging downpour.

Of course.

With my hand over my head, I dashed across the remaining five meters of pavement that separated me from the overhang of a nearby building.

The parish center. At last.

I stood with pride. Rebecca the Klutz had not fallen down once, even with watery impediment. Good. Peter did not deserve the satisfaction of discovering otherwise.

I reached for the doorknob.

It was a small, cozy room with a few chairs scattered about for visitors. A receptionist was seated at a deep mahogany desk, the home to assorted papers and a neatly-arranged container of writing utensils. Behind the desk was a short hall down which one might find four offices, one for each of the parish priests.

I hesitated, and then approached the front desk.

"Hey, Mary Katharine!"

"Hi, Rebecca!" she responded cheerfully. She was an amiable woman, tall and middle-aged with short brown hair and an eternally peaceful countenance. I wished for such a peaceful countenance right about then.

I cleared my throat for what I hoped would be the last time that day. "I seem to have misplaced—"

My words were cut short when I heard the shuffling of a new pair of feet in the vicinity.

"Oh, hi, Rebecca. Imagine seeing you here."

Grey robes, held together by a long, white rope. Simple brown sandals. A slightly balding head.

Father D'Angelo stood, a short, jolly man with round rosy cheeks like Santa Claus on Christmas morning. He was the spitting image of a Franciscan friar. And I realized, at that moment, that the Franciscan friar was the true Santa Claus.

I also realized that, at the moment, there was something in Father D'Angelo's twinkling brown eyes that made me rather suspicious.

"Hi, Father D'Angelo," I smiled.

He had expected me, obviously. He doesn't...does he?

"Would you mind coming to my office for a moment?"

I nodded, following him down the hallway. I could not get the image out of my mind of the one time I had been sent to the principal's office in high school. I had been sitting innocently in Spanish class, the last period of the day, when I was unexpectedly summoned to the office. Completely bewildered by the puzzling phone call—as were my fellow students, who viewed me as a goody-two-shoes and proceeded to stare at me for several moments in disbelief—I rose from my seat, my face growing warm, and walked in a daze to the door. I remember the long walk to the office, a march filled with dread, but, mostly, confusion. When I arrived, I discovered that I had been called as a witness in regards to the identification of the individual who had thrown a battery to the front of the room in fourth period biology class earlier that day.

Witness? The irony of my recollections in conjunction with the present-day scenario in which I found myself almost made me laugh.

I did not laugh, however, when Father D'Angelo opened the door, escorting me in, and the first item that my eyes took in was a rather unremarkable, average-sized, woven brown basket, underlined with scarlet felt, on his comparably substantial desk.

Father D'Angelo casually strolled over to said desk, reached into the basket as if he were the announcer of a prize-winning contestant, and pulled out an equally insignificant-looking scrap of folded paper.

Of course.

"Is this what you were looking for?" he inquired, holding up the note, his bright eyes dancing.

I groaned. "You didn't...*read* it, did you?"

"We'll just call it confidential Confession material."

My face must have betrayed some sense of bewilderment and horror because, in the next moment, I watched Father D'Angelo shake his head with a smile.

"No, I didn't. It has your name on it."

I let out a sigh of relief, extending my hand for that

persnickety piece of paper that Father D'Angelo held out to me. *That persnickety piece of paper that had successfully eluded me for so long, but had finally been captured.*

Sure enough, my full name, *Rebecca Elizabeth Veritas*, was written on the outside of the folded paper. *I wonder who else noticed that.* Or who might have been less tactful than the parish priest.

"Thank you, Father D'Angelo." I hesitated, feeling the need to explain myself at least partially. "It's just a note from one of your ushers."

*Wow...**that** was smooth.*

"You're welcome," he smiled, escorting me down the hall to the entrance. Curiosity regarding the note escalating rapidly, I walked quickly to the door.

"Let me know when you want to make an appointment for Engaged Encounter."

"Very funny, Father."

I halted at the door as a flash of silver suddenly captured my attention. My eyes took in the necklace that I was wearing, a silver chain holding the image of a delicate seashell. *A creamy white seashell that reminded me of the moon.*

It had been a gift from Father D'Angelo, given to me at our annual Christmas party the year I had turned eleven. He had told me, with that special smile of his, that it had reminded him of me.

I looked back up, looked at Father D'Angelo, who stood there, smiling.

Oh, forget it. Dropping my hand from the doorknob, I ran like a small child to her favorite uncle to throw my arms around the jolly friar's neck. *The jolly friar who I secretly called Friar Tuck due to the uncanny resemblance between the two.* He received it with a deep-throated chuckle, a chuckle that spoke of the merriment of Christmastime and the timelessness of a seagull's cry to the never-ending union of sea and land.

I had known Father D'Angelo since I was six, and he was family. I understood by my connection to him the closeness that Dad felt towards Monsignor McGregor. He was like one big heart, joyfully beating to the sound of a music that many had long forgotten. *A heart that, through this joy—the greatest sense of joy— knew peace and, by that peace, was able to perceive that which many failed to recognize.*

A heart that saw into the heart.

I moved back to watch one of Father D'Angelo's teasing, yet knowing, smiles and, with that contagious joy now entering my heart, I moved towards the door.

"Ciao, Father."

"Ciao, bambina," he replied, completing a customary farewell between two Italians.

As I closed the door behind me, devising various strategies of reprimanding Peter for the juvenile behavior that I secretly appreciated, I came to a sudden stop.

I had crashed into a familiar figure with wisps of white hair and knowing gray eyes.

Of course.

And it had stopped raining as suddenly as it had begun.

His eyes met mine.

I muttered my apologies to Cedric and sped off to read my note.

As I reached the family car, a slightly-worn, white Mazda, I caught sight of my mom approaching from the direction of the chapel. I stood, waiting, tapping my foot impatiently against the drying pavement as I stared at The Note. At *it*.

After all this hassle to get it, after all of my innate curiosity enhanced by this anomalous occurrence, something still told me to *wait*.

We got in the car, rolled down the windows, and snapped on our seatbelts.

Not yet.

The purr of the car reached a lion's roar.

Almost.

Reverse to Forward. Mom backed out of the parking space and began to speed ahead.

*Okay, **now**.*

I unfolded the note labeled, "Rebecca Elizabeth Veritas." It read as follows:

My most esteemed Rebecca,

I would be honored if you would join me for an evening of writing exercises at 7 PM one day hence. That is, of course, if your homework is defeated first.

Most cordially,
Your servant,
Peter Joseph Asturian

That was it?!

I shook my head, smiling, as I re-folded the note. *Well, what had I expected?*

The momentum of the car suddenly seemed to undergo a significant change. I looked up just in time to note yet another familiar figure walking towards the car.

Of course.

Mom lowered my window.

Peter Joseph Asturian stood, grinning from ear to ear.

I waved the piece of paper in front of his face.

"You could have just sent me an email."

Chapter Nineteen

Te

"If you lived back in medieval times, what sort of person would you be?" I mused, tapping my pen against the keyboard of the family computer. I still couldn't decide whether I preferred to use the more old-fashioned pen or the modern computer for writing. It really seemed to depend on my mood.

"Random, no?" Peter grinned.

"The usual," I grinned back.

"Well," he looked into space as if lost in thought, "I suppose I'd like to be a juggler. A court jester or something of the sort. That way, I would appear to be a fool, but really learn all the court secrets."

His smiling eyes returned to me. "And you? A princess no doubt…?"

"Ha, ha. Actually, I think that it would be fascinating to be a bard."

"Oh?" Peter raised an eyebrow in interest.

"Allow me to brainstorm aloud…?"

He nodded, the usual Peter-Is-Trying-To-Keep-A-Straight-Face smile beginning to weave its way across his face. *The smile that never ridiculed my ideas, but always seemed to find amusement at how I presented them.*

"Well," I began slowly, "I would travel far and wide…seeing, listening, creating. I would weave tales for an enthralled audience. A song would be heard throughout the kingdom, and I would be a part of that. You would normally think that a bard would pick up his tales from stories heard in his travels or, perhaps, from personal observation of these events. Perhaps some bards would create the stories themselves or, at least, adapt the original versions heard."

Peter nodded, his eyes thoughtful.

"But what if the bard were really more than a bard?" I continued eagerly. "What if he were once a gallant knight or an old sea captain…perhaps even a forgotten prince? What if the stories he told, what if the characters brought to life in his stories, were really of his comrades and himself? Stories from long ago that he finally wished to be heard? What if those who listened to his tales, all the while assuming that they were far disconnected from their communicator, were really listening to the narrative of a wanderer intimately connected to it all? And where would such an individual go when his final days as an "official" bard were spent? Perhaps he would decide to retire in a lighthouse. For, surely, no place would be more fitting for the hero emeritus. He would gaze upon the glorious sea in recollection…guiding others with the beacon of light atop his home as he had once been shepherded. The adventurer became the storyteller…and then the Sentinel of the Sea.

"Or, maybe," I finished, finally shaking myself from a dream-like trance, "I need to get over my rambling tendencies." I looked back at Peter and grinned.

"You know, Rebecca," Peter said, as he returned to reality—for, he, too, had been staring thoughtfully into space—"You really are a poet."

I grinned, "You mean, it wasn't cliché?"

"Hardly."

"Good."

There was a slight pause in the conversation. But, then, suddenly, Peter sat up straight.

"What?" I asked excitedly. Once again, I was reminded of the random escapades so often shared with Adriana.

"Do you know who would like to meet our sea bard?"

"Who?!"

His eyes told me that I should know the answer, yet I was clueless.

"Think *Intermission*."

Realization dawned upon me. *GMTA.*

"Antonio!"

"The story within the story version," Peter finished.

"Monet is going to be really mad at us," I grinned.

A scene from "Muse"
Written by Morena

Antonio blinked rapidly. Only a few moments earlier he had been standing in the spacious room of a chandelier-lit castle. Now he was outside...outside on the shore of a moonlit beach, his hair caught imploringly by zephyrs of wind. He watched as waves chased each other in a never-ending dance, laughing, smiling, **being***. It was youthful yet solemn, calm yet turbulent. It was eternity at a glance.*

And completely mesmerizing*, Antonio thought, as he sat down, unable to turn away from the sea. It was as if he were hypnotized, yet there was too great a truth to this world of sea and sand for any human influence to come into question. And, as he gazed into the beyond, he suddenly understood that he was* **home***.*

It had not been often that he had had the opportunity to visit the coast; his home was deep within the mainland, a world of forests, a world of mystery, yet not the same peace. And, whenever he had traveled hence, it had seemed that there was always something more pressing that required his attention...a game of ball, a race along the shore, a race across the sea. Always moving, always turning, always reaching and searching but never quite seeking, never quite

being. At that moment, the two words, searching and seeking, seemed so utterly distinctive, so completely different, like opposites in this world of absolutes. Everything seemed so clear to him here, in this serene, almost mystical place. It was surreal, yet so entirely real. He tasted Truth, a truth that he could not put into words. But this place was his sanctuary. This he knew. This he knew without question.

He bent down to unfasten the laces of his dark shoes. They were black, black as the night before him, yet light was cast softly upon their smooth surface in such a way that no distinctive color could be identified by the eye. **Black against the pale glow of a creamy white moon.**

He wished to be more like the sea. He wished to know its wisdom, its peace. He wished to know the legend that it spoke. The legend that soared far beyond legends. The Legend that spoke Truth.

His feet played catch with the light sprinkling of sand beneath his feet as he watched the sun descend onto the waiting waves. **Moment by moment, closer, closer, until the waves were glittering sapphires on the canvas of the Great Painter.** Splashes of color grew, touched by invisible hands, shining forth above and below, a beauty that could not be contained, not be for half a world alone. **Sky and sea, sea and shore, together, united in an eternal caress.**

Sun? How could the sun set when the moon has already presented itself? he wondered.

No matter. It was here. **Time was here.**

With a great sigh that may come only when one has witnessed the greatest beauty the world has to offer, Antonio pulled himself up from the sand-scattered surface and began to walk as if in a dream. How long he walked, he did not know—minutes, hours, days—all he knew was that he would not like anything better than to continue forth in this way forever. All senses became one—the sound of seagulls chattering in the distance, the smell of salt air filling his nostrils with sweet, heavenly delight, the gentle caress of a sea breeze, the sight of dazzling sparkles amidst a blue-green world of tumbling waves outlined in soft, delicate lace.

Yet, as the beach darkened with the approaching nightfall, so did the coolness surrounding him intensify—still refreshing, still true, but too strong for a mere mortal to withstand.

It was time to find shelter.

Antonio began to walk backwards, not wishing to lose sight of the sea, for as long as he could before falling, sprawling, into the sand. He arose, brushing off sand as he went, and finally began to walk forward to his unknown destination. Yet he could not help looking back every few moments as the sun grew smaller and smaller, the sunset reaching the climax of its glory, the peak of its fullness, the final note of tapestry's song.

He remembered. In his mind's eye, he saw the vision of a child, as he was years before, running down the dunes to catch his first sight of the sea, his first sight of home. He had forgotten somehow…forgotten in the ebb and flow, the buzz of daily life. **Forgotten his existence in life, the life in existence.** He would not like to forget again, he thought, as the last few inches of his beach receded from his vision.

It was then that Antonio started, finding himself face-to-face with another beacon of light.

It was a lighthouse.

And a lighthouse so close that he had almost run into it.

Antonio had heard tell of these professed havens of the sea from wayward travelers to his homeland, been witness to spellbinding tales of how this reassuring, yet mysterious, beam of light had saved sailors from certain death...yet an encounter with one himself was something else altogether.

Reassuring, yet mysterious. *Antonio realized that the lighthouse reminded him of the sea itself. Indeed, it watched over the seas and brought weary travelers home to their loved ones. And brought tales...tales of the sea.*

The lighthouse stood, waiting, waiting for something, or someone. **Waiting for him.**

And, so, he followed its call, stepping forward to tap lightly on the large, wooden door.

Antonio had barely lifted his hand from its surface when it burst open.

He was old, yet young. *Stark white hair came in billows about his wrinkled face. Dark grey eyes gazed down at him intently with the wisdom of the ages. Yet there was a youthfulness in those eyes, a merriment concealed behind the solemn poise of its wearer.*

He was timeless.

He was dressed in a long white shift which blew about him in the wind of the night. Antonio realized with embarrassment that he had likely interrupted his sleep, yet knew, at the same time, that the old man, like the lighthouse, like the sea, had been waiting for him.

Yet Antonio was the member of a polite society, and, so, he began to open his mouth to mutter an apology. Halfway through his fumbling words, the owner of the lighthouse raised one hand, shaking his head, as if to indicate that further explanation was unnecessary. He pointed to the open door and, without a word, walked through it. Antonio stood, bewildered, for a few moments in the doorway, uncertain how to proceed. He understood through the lighthouse keeper's silent directions that he was to follow. Yet, he hesitated. He had no idea what lay beyond that door. He had no reason to trust that man. And yet he did. An inexplicable trust had formed the instant he had set foot on that sand-scattered shore. And that sense of trust had not abandoned him when the lighthouse suddenly, as if by magic, had appeared before him. Nor did it disappear when he met its silent proprietor.

So, whether he liked it or not—and it admittedly gave him comfort—he trusted it...trusted it all. With a strange, yet satisfying, peace filling his entire being, Antonio closed his eyes, stepping forth blind to enter the great, mysterious lighthouse.

Antonio: Dreamy!

Elise: Awesome!

Monet: Zephyrs?!

Chapter Twenty

Contemplans

It was the fifth Sunday of Lent.

I began to cough uncontrollably.

"You okay?" Peter asked, his brow creased in concern. We were at our usual location at the back of the church, moving in and out with the flow of traffic. Mass had ended only a couple of minutes earlier.

"Yeah, it's just," I waved my hand as another wave of coughing overtook me, "my asthma. I developed it last month when I got pneumonia."

I looked down, biting my lip.

"I hate it," I said fiercely, with more bitterness than I had intended.

Peter nodded, his eyes large and sympathetic. "I have asthma, too…ever since I was a kid."

"Really?" For some reason, that made me feel a little better. *Misery loves company, I guess*, I thought to myself. *Only, with Peter, it somehow went deeper than that.*

"So, that makes you," I paused, "M.A.B."

"M.A.B.?" Peter raised an eyebrow.

"My Asthma Buddy," I grinned.

"Ah…but, of course," Peter returned the grin. Then, his face grew more thoughtful, the contours lining it more serious.

"My asthma's gotten much better," his voice rose with pride.

He looked at me.

"As it will with you."

Waves of warmth, reminiscent of a day not too long before, filled my chest. I smiled, not knowing what to say.

"Thank you," I finally managed, my voice barely audible. I looked up at Peter, and his confidence suddenly became my own.

Then I began to cough again.

I grimaced in frustration.

"Do you have an inhaler?" Peter asked softly, sympathy filling his voice.

"Yeah…in my bag here." I felt in my purse for the correct shape. When my hand finally found the inhaler, I pulled it out, eyeing it with a mixture of relief and distaste.

A buzz of chatter ensued as another wave of people neared the back of the church. I motioned towards the community room, and Peter followed.

I removed the medicine from the aero chamber and examined it tentatively. "I've only used it a few times…and once with the doctor's help," I explained apologetically. "I guess I know how to use it, but still feel kinda weird about it." I paused. "You shake it first, right?"

In a different situation, I would have expected Peter's reaction to my confusion to be humorous. He might have teased me about my ignorance. And I would not have rebuked him for it. *But he did not now.*

"Here," Peter motioned for me to hand it to him.

I handed him both parts of the inhaler.

My heart warmed as I noticed his face remained unchanged as he examined the inhaler. He knew that this moment was serious for me.

And that meant a lot to me.

He shook the canister and reinserted it, beckoning for me to move closer.

I began to move forward, but then I hesitated.

"You don't have to…"

Peter waved my words away.

I placed my lips over the mouthpiece.

Peter pressed the canister down and began to count quietly, soothingly.

1001

The thought crossed my mind that the medicine tasted slightly like persimmons…or some warped version of the fruit. I resisted the urge to laugh.

1002

I looked at Peter, holding the inhaler. *Standing there,*

tall and confident.

1003

I instinctively grasped his shoulder. He reached out his hand and squeezed mine. His eyes, calm and earnest, held me and encouraged me.

I felt…safe.

1004

And calm.

1005

I exhaled slowly and then began to breathe in the medicine again…calmly, slowly.

MicroExpress: 60 seconds.

It was 3 AM, and a persistent whistle from within had brought me, eyes half-closed, head pounding, out of my comfortable bed.

I sat down, a cup of apple juice tingling with warmth in one hand. Then, almost as an afterthought, a wave of emotion overtook me and I leaned over to the nearest drawer, pulling out a pen…

Beautiful

I sit, not knowing what to write
Yet feeling
    a word
       Beautiful.
          wings outstretched

I Thirst

gliding
> singing
>> dreaming

I shiver.
> They wrap around me.
>> pulling me from
>>> clinging
>>>> shadows

> Not letting me
>> fall

I stumble, my head
> spinning
Gently, they steady me.
I collapse,
> encompassed by the
>> Everything.

Golden Mast
> shining forth

A warm embrace
> Catches fallen tears
I bury my face deeper
> deeper
And smile.
Beautiful.
You are Beautiful.

A scene from "Muse"
Written by Morena

When he opened his eyes once again, he was caught in wonder.

This was no ordinary lighthouse, such as the ones he had read about in books and heard described in the tales of old sailors, as romantic and wondrous as those had always seemed to him. Nothing could have prepared him for the sight that awaited him.

His eyes were instantly drawn to a great fountain at the center of the small room. Yet, as Antonio gazed at this enchanting whirlpool of beauty, he realized that it was not a fountain at all, but the abode of splashing waves. It was more ocean than fountain, more free than contained. And yet it was neither. Waves gracefully spun around in a circular dance, reaching halfway to the high ceiling of the lighthouse. And around this great sea-pool were rows upon rows of roses — an array of many colors, some nameless to the eye — too numerous to count as they swirled elegantly around the water.

Antonio turned to examine the rest of the house more closely. Shelves donned nearly every corner like exquisite drapes, filled with books, musical instruments — lyres, fiddles, and some that he could not identify — seashells — all curves of pink and white and gray—sentinels guarding watch. A few chairs lay scattered about, as well as a roughly hewn, sparse bed and a simple wooden table that looked rather plain next to such splendor. Opposite the doorway in which he stood was a large round hole, portal to the sea. While it interrupted the flow of lightly colored stone that formed the walls, it hardly seemed to be an interruption; it was merely a variation on a theme. It was spun seamlessly into the framework. A great telescope stood near this portal, and to the right of this, worn wooden steps that lead to the top of the lighthouse, to the sanctuary of the light itself.

The keeper of the lighthouse motioned for Antonio to sit down in a chair adjacent to a small table laden with assorted things of the sea, from rocks and shells to starfish. Antonio stood, uncertain again; this man was much older than he. It would be improper for him to sit if the other man did not. But one sharp look from the old lighthouse keeper impelled him to sit down in a hurry.

As Antonio approached the chair, he noticed that it received warmth from a brightly burning fire that lay near. Such a fire might bring warmth to travelers; in that respect, it was a rather ordinary addition to the room. Yet it was strange that Antonio had not noticed the fire before and stranger still that water and flame coexisted so peacefully in this place.

The chair creaked loudly as he sat down; the thought crossed his mind that the piece of furniture could be as old as the owner himself.

The lighthouse keeper remained standing, gazing through a small porthole at the sea beyond. Several minutes passed in silence, the crackling of the fire and the occasional creaking of the Antonio's chair as he shifted his feet the only sounds in an otherwise quiet room.

"Many a year I traveled those seas," he finally said, unmoving, his eyes forever cast ahead. "Many a year I told her tales. And then the time came for me to watch. And watch I have."

He turned towards Antonio with a smile, "She never changes, does she?"

The sea.

"No, I don't suppose she does."

The sentinel of the sea bent down near the whirlpool — the sea fountain, fountain sea — and plucked one of the deep red roses surrounding it. It was then that Antonio realized with a start that the roses were not from a field or garden somewhere far away. They grew inside of the lighthouse, through what appeared to be a simple wooden floor.

Well, oceans don't normally sprout up in the middle of a room either, *he told himself with a wry smile, shaking his head with a mixture of incredulity and awe.*

The old sea captain walked slowly to Antonio, finally sitting down in the chair directly across from him.

"Tell me, boy, what does this remind you of?" he said, his eyes penetrating, as he handed him the rose, a beauty in full bloom.

For a moment, Antonio stared ahead dreamily, as if lost in some fantastical world.

"My Patria," he finally said, a smile as full as the rose in his hand filling his countenance.

The old man's eyes spoke, "Homeland. And what kind of homeland is this? A girl, perhaps?" *He gazed ahead once again, his thoughts lost in time, as if recalling something, or someone.*

His voice was quiet, yet earnest. "Yes. My love. The lady who owns my heart and will soon be my bride."

"Aye, you are a lucky one then, lad," the old sea captain said thoughtfully.

Antonio smiled, "I suppose I am."

The old man moved his hand slowly to the table beside them, grasping a small, delicate seashell, and, with a surprisingly firm grip, handed it to Antonio.

"And what do you suppose these two," he gestured to the rose and the shell, "have in common? Do they...sing the same song?"

A tangible silence once again wrapped itself around the small, yet immense, lighthouse as Antonio scrupulously examined the two items.

The old sea captain shook his head. "Don't try so hard, boy. Feel your way around it."

Antonio closed his eyes and lightly outlined the rose's petals with one finger for a few moments. He then opened them, placing the flower carefully in his lap, and took the shell into the same hand. He began to trace its smooth form in thoughtful silence. He opened his eyes once again, holding up the rose and the shell, an object in each hand.

"They are each a maze," he said thoughtfully. "Each of them—both the rose and the shell—go around and around in their own way, yet each of them has—"

"A center," the old sea captain finished, watching Antonio.

*At these words, Antonio's eyes were suddenly drawn to the blue-green whirlpool of light at the center of the room. **A small sea, a microcosm of the ocean...waves splashing***

delightfully toward one central focal point.

He suddenly understood without understanding what he had never quite comprehended before—always caught in snapshots and glimpses, but never entirely, never fully, understood.

Antonio turned towards the sea captain again, whose face was aglow with a brilliant, yet subtle, smile, a moon of a smile, for it was too quiet to know the sun directly, but remained just as beautiful. Full of light, glorious, serene, **alive**. And suddenly Antonio was pulled towards that great whirlpool, closer and closer, yet he was not afraid. The waves closed over him just as he turned to observe the old sea captain put on a straw hat in the shape of a cone...

Elise: That was super interesting!

Antonio: Symbolic! Full of meaning! Wondrous!

Monet: Seashell?! Rose?! A moon of a smile?!

Chapter Twenty-One

Totum

She reminded me of the Abominable Snowman. Not that I had ever met him, but I instantly knew that this was it. A coldness, nearly tangible due to its extreme weight, was perceptible the instant I entered the room. The sharpness of her chin and the geometric precision of dark glasses atop a piercingly angular nose only seemed to add to her frigid demeanor.

Adriana always said that I tended to have strong first impressions, asserting that I was usually right. Not that I didn't give the person another chance. Yet I did not often find myself making such harsh judgments as I had just initiated. Thus, as I approached the secretary's desk, I began to wonder if there was not some truth to my conclusions.

"Hi, I'm here to have a test proctored," I stated politely.

She looked up briefly and surveyed me with a cool glance. "Last name?"

"Veritas."

She looked up again, this time staring at me for a long moment. In that moment, I felt that I was being completely scrutinized in a way that was the exact opposite of that which I experienced when Peter gazed at me. He saw deep within me and she saw neither outside nor within. Uneasiness overtook me and I attempted to avert my eyes.

I blinked, trying to regain my composure. But another element that I had not foreseen entered the mix.

I began to cough. It was a cough that I felt deep within my chest and, when I finally caught my breath, a sickeningly sweet scent that was too sweet to be real filled my nostrils.

Air freshener.

So *that* was what had also filled my chest. Cinnamon, lavender, or orange, I would know that scent—anywhere. *An artificial replacement for the real, the authentic. Fakery found in the aisle of the local grocery store. A commodity filled with carcinogens that penetrated every wall like a plague.* And a plague to which I happened to be personally and incredibly sensitive.

I cleared my throat, as the typical congestion began to control all of my senses.

I reluctantly turned back to the Abominable Snowwoman. "This probably will sound like a weird question." My words trailed off.

She looked up sharply, a barely perceptible nod seeming to indicate that I might continue.

I knew from experience how defensive people could get about their air fresheners, so I chose my next words carefully.

"Is there, by any chance, air freshener here? I actually am really allergic to it."

Abominable Snowwoman stared coldly at me.

"Sorry for the inconvenience," I continued nervously. "I did call beforehand; one of the assistants assured me that air freshener was not used in this facility."

"You don't like the sea breeze?"

Her words were icy, detached, and would have almost been robotic if it had not been for the pulsing consciousness at their very center.

"I love the real thing," I said cheerfully. Despite my personal feelings, I managed to speak in what I felt was a chatty, conversational tone.

And it probably was. But she did not seem like the chatty, conversational type.

"It is only in my office. The testing facility does not have air freshener."

"Got it! Thanks!" I replied enthusiastically.

She continued to stare at me.

"You will put your belongings in the rack to your left," she finally said briskly. "You will take out two Number 2 pencils to use for the test. You will sit in Seat

#15 for the duration of the exam."

"Okay!" I approached the shelf and unloaded my purse and sweater. I dug into my purse for the pencils that I had put in there that morning. I retrieved three pencils and a pink eraser.

"*Two* pencils." A disembodied voice spoke sharply from behind me.

I put one pencil back in my purse, zipping up the compartment from which it came.

Was she actually making me put back a pencil because it was one too many?

"No gum in the testing facility."

I held up my eraser for her to see. "It's actually an eraser."

"Hmph."

She handed me the green test booklet. It looked like a summer leaf, but reminded me more of a moldy dungeon.

Strange. I didn't usually get wrapped into uneasiness before a test, over-prepared as I tended to be.

I made my way to an alternative entrance opposite the one behind her desk. It would enable me to avoid the air freshener. *The less pollution in my lungs, the better.*

"Stop."

I stopped, nearly throwing my hands up, to observe the Abominable Snowwoman eyeing me as if she had just caught me stealing her most prized possession.

Her most prized possession? Probably sea breeze air freshener.

She really had nothing to fear.

"You will enter the door behind my desk to take the exam. The other door is for employees only."

She did not raise her voice, but her words held eerie power. *A power found in icy detachment.*

"Okay," I managed to say. *Tone alteration: from conversational and chatty to meek acceptance.*

I glanced at the other entrance before leaving. *Funny. I didn't see the usual "Employees Only" sign on the door.*

I began to have a sick, sinking feeling at the bottom of my stomach.

As I turned the knob, holding my breath as I passed by the air freshener affixed mockingly to the left of the new door, I could have sworn that I heard a snort from behind me.

Once inside, I began my search for Seat #15. I finally spotted it on the far right of the room next to…

No window.

Odd.

Usually there would be a window of some sort right about there in the typical classroom.

Not that it mattered.

I sat down behind the desk labeled #15, placing my eraser in a strategic position to avoid any freefall action on the part of my pencils, and gently released the testing booklet from the translucent sticker holding the pages together.

I surveyed my surroundings. No one else was there. *Different.* Not the school scene I was used to, but it would provide a nice and quiet environment in which to take the exam.

I picked up my pencil, and coughed.

I had learned two things in my unfortunate history of air freshener encounters: 1) Limited exposure could result in unlimited effects. I recalled an instance a few months prior in which I had washed my hands quickly in a school restroom filled with air freshener. I was only there for a few minutes and, thus, did not take the exposure seriously. In other words, my usual beeline to the shower upon arriving home did not occur. *Bad move.* I had one of my worst asthma attacks that night. Thus, at this moment, I could just be experiencing the aftermath of the office exposure. 2) Air freshener permeates the entire room in which it is "officially" present and often its surroundings...like a great enveloping cloud. A person would only have to leave the door of the testing facility slightly ajar for the scent to seep through the framework to the next room. Therefore, I could be inhaling "secondhand" air freshener right now.

But I had to take a test. A U.S. history final for which I had studied long and hard. I would not be impeded. I would plunge my way through and make it. The test would take no longer than two hours, surely, and then I would be home free.

I began the test. Yet, as I worked my way through the multiple choice and essay questions, my vision began to blur as a wave of dizziness overwhelmed me. I blinked, attempting to sort out the confusion in my head, but finding myself unable to shake off the feeling of disorientation. Bouts of nausea overtook me amidst the sealing off of my nose from its normal routine, a process that grew more rapid by the second. My throat was raw, burning as if from some unseen sore. But all of these symptoms paled in comparison to the scariest of them all, the violent throbbing in my chest. Every time I breathed in, the pain intensified. And, with each breath, a distinctive whistling sound from deep within my chest informed me that I was wheezing pretty badly.

I was not breathing normally.

It was as if all central systems of my body had shut down. It was "I am Sick" by Shel Silverstein, only the state of affairs was all too real.

But I had to continue. I tried to distract myself from my physical discomfort by focusing my complete and full attention on the test.

Okay, Rebecca, Question #15. You can do this.

Yet, I became more and more disoriented by the minute.

The War of 1812

Watergate

The Battle of Gettysburg

John Jay

the year 1600

dove around my brain cells, dodging my queries, laughing as if it were all a game.

But it was not a game. It was not a game at all.

It was as if someone were sucking each kernel of knowledge from my brain, one by one.

A comparison that would sound funny if it were not so pathetic.

I could not think. Schemata were in complete and total disarray. My organized mind had turned into a garbled mess.

I could not concentrate.

But I would have to.

I willed myself to continue, to focus, staring at the page before me with such intensity as to will *it* to retrieve my knowledge, my understanding of my country. Yet, a detail that normally would have taken approximately one minute to recall was extracted by force after fifteen long minutes. And the deeper meaning behind it all left me in a hazy fog.

It didn't make sense. *The world* didn't make sense.

I nearly collapsed onto the wooden desk before me, my body completely fatigued. I was tired of fighting this battle.

I resisted the urge to steal a look at the clock behind me. I knew that I was taking more time than I would have under more healthy circumstances.

I had a class to attend later that day.

Later. **Now** *is probably later,* I thought to myself bitterly.

No, Rebecca. Focus on the test. That is all that matters at the moment. Believe that, and you will be fine. Will yourself to continue. You're almost done.

Will myself to continue? I shouldn't have to will myself to continue. I shouldn't have to take a test while I'm having an allergic reaction. I shouldn't have to work when I cannot breathe.

But you are only a paragraph away from the end of the last essay.

I could tell someone that I'm having trouble breathing.

Who? The Abominable Snowwoman? She won't care.

You're right. She won't.

I sighed, the wheezing deep within my chest the only sound in the silence of that cold room.

This is going to be the worst concluding paragraph that I have ever written.

Don't think about that now. Besides, it's a truth universally acknowledged that all concluding paragraphs of in-class essays are poorly written.

Oh, go away. Leave me here to die.

No, Rebecca. Fight it. Fight it just a bit longer.

And, so, with the persistence of my inner dialogue, two parts of me battling away, I coughed my way through the rest of the exam.

With a sigh of relief that I instantly chastised myself for—as it brought on another tirade of coughing fits—I closed my testing booklet. I sat for a few moments, too tired to get up, too tired to even move. I finally tilted my head slightly to glance at the clock behind me. Three and a half hours had raced by as I dumbly stared down a series of test questions. Class was in half an hour. *Great.*

As I pushed my chair in, something drew my eyes upward.

Directly above Seat #15, placed with strategic precision in a completely symmetrical manner, was a skin-colored, plug-in air freshener.

My trusting nature had not foreseen Possibility #3: Air freshener in testing facility. Air freshener placed right above student seat. *A lie.*

My eyes continued their walk about the room, searching for similar devices placed above or near any of the other seats. As far as I could tell, there were no other air fresheners in the room, no other plug-ins planted above any of the other seats.

Just Seat #15. My assigned seat.

I shuffled my feet, walking slowly, as if in a trance, to the door. I moved my hand forward to open it.

She looked up, a sardonic smile playing upon her lips.

"So, you survived?"

I did not answer, silently holding out my test booklet for her to collect.

She took it. I did not stop to watch her cold face change, or stay the same, or do whatever it was that it was to do. I did not wish to know what it would do.

I mechanically slipped my two Number 2 pencils and eraser into my purse.

When I reached the door, I turned back to look her straight in the eye.

"You must live in a very cold world."

And, without a second thought, I closed the door.

I had not aced the test, that I knew. After all of those hours of studying, I would be lucky if I did not blow my "A" in the class.

But, right now, only half of me could care. Only half of Rebecca the Perfectionist, and that part of me was tired. A wave of dizziness overtook me. I tried to breathe in deeply, but I could only cough. I felt so weak.

I reached into the outer compartment of my purse and mechanically dialed Alex's number. I barely remembered telling him that I had finished the test and then stood quietly, waiting outside in the dim light of dusk.

I stood, my mind wiped of any coherent thought but that of getting into my brother's car and leaving this place.

I shivered, pulling my sweater more tightly around me.

How cold humanity could be.

I stood, an eight-year-old who just wanted to "go home."

It was…beautiful.

Beautiful. You are Beautiful.

I pulled the sweater closer, wrapping Peter's words—and my own—around me.

What happened next was a blur. I opened the door. I heard my mom's

voice

calling my name

coming forward with a smile

and then seeing her smile replaced

by a line of worry

across her brow

I, dumbly trying

to explain

but only wanting to

breathe

chest throbbing

in agony

She told me that I wasn't up to going to my

night class

that a shower

would do wonders

as I nodded, stumbling

falling

collapsing

in her outstretched arms

as everything suddenly

went black

Fresh
Rebecca Elizabeth Veritas

You are here
And so am I
We can't both be here

I Thirst

At the same time
I cannot see you
At least, at first
But I know you're here
and you thirst.

A siren call allowed to ring
Throughout the world
You roam free.
Leading the unaware
To the deadly depths below.

My chest is victim
Carried deep
A knife shrieks loudly
Pounces in a single leap
My lungs torn and scattered wide
I live without them
They are yours
No longer mine.
I am a half-filled vessel
With lungs cast aside.

I slowly slip into the shadows
My head, whirling,
Grasps a single shadow
The shadow of a drawing

A 1-D image once 3-D
You've turned me into a paper doll.
And a paper doll cannot breathe.

Oh inTOXICatingly fresh scent!
Air freshener
You take my breath away.

Micro Express: 30 seconds.
Welcome Back.
A solitary visitor of the night.
If that wasn't cliché, that is.
I sipped the hot apple juice carefully, my eyes burning with fatigue.

He understood. He cared. And, even if Peter did not have asthma, I somehow knew that he would still understand. And care.

I rubbed my eyes. A movie reel flashed before my eyes as I remembered my previous encounters with air "fresheners," as I recalled other asthma attacks.

I groaned, remembering that, while sleep would bring some refuge, my chest might still feel tight when I woke up in the morning, that the stubborn weakness that swept through my body now would probably linger throughout the following day. But I would be okay; I would be okay. And, if I were not okay, I could talk to Peter.

I probably would not say much. I would want to,

but the difficulty of the subject for me, coupled with hesitation, coupled with a lack of desire to come off as a whining nuisance, would keep me from saying everything. But, I would say *something*. I would say something, and he would not ask for more. He would read between the lines. He would read my heart more than my words. And, most importantly, he would *listen*.

It was with this thought that I closed my eyes, still seated in that old, rickety chair, unaware of when my dad, hours later, came to the kitchen to find me fast asleep.

A scene from "Muse"
Written by Elise

…and he was back.

The aroma of freshly baked bread delicately departed from its surface. The scent was the sight; the sight, the sound. An array of varied waves circled in an overwhelming ecstasy of emotion, swirling in carefully paced delight. It was a walk, it was a chase, it was a **symphony of time**.

Antonio quietly placed the cover over the great instrument. He closed his eyes, smiling as he recalled the newly-held triumph. The rays of the sun escaped from the nearby window, gently caressing his bright, deep brown eyes with light.

"I don't understand," he thought, "how such is possible! This is just a slightly more advanced wooden box with a variety of sound vibrations. How does it make travel to another world possible?"

"Well," he admitted to himself, "not so easily. Nor so quickly. This piece has enveloped my mind for days."

"But," he thought with a start, "it is as if it has always been there." He was now speaking aloud, rubbing his sweaty brow which was also covered with dirt that he had long forgotten. "But it isn't here…it's very much somewhere else…a forgotten land on no recorded map," he mused.

The sound of someone—a familiar someone—clearing her throat took him from his inner thoughts.

The piano's shining black and white keys glistened and curled into the swirls of movement that Antonio had so recently visited. Below, two warm, dark eyes smiled at him with love, and a bit of humor. His love. His Patria.

"Still in the stars, my love?" She stood in the doorway, an eyebrow raised in vague amusement.

Antonio smiled, knowing the truth of her eyes that could not be hidden. "Today and forevermore."

She smiled, attempting to maintain the mock disapproval on her countenance. With this pretense, she glided gracefully to sit next to Antonio on the piano bench.

"Am I to wed one or receive two in the act?" she grinned openly. "You have already said your vows to one," she continued, indicating the great pianoforte with a wave of her hand.

Antonio grinned back, accustomed to this game. "We are but one."

"And soon three shall be one."

"No, only two, for one is but the other."

His face grew serious. He gazed at Patria, a gentle caress filling his eyes.

"You are the only music of my heart."

Patria snorted overtly, peals of laughter filling the small room. But, as she turned almost bashfully away, Antonio once again knew.

"Only you can say such foolishness beautifully," she said softly, turning her eyes back to her beloved.

"I am content to be such a fool by your side."

Patria looked down in an attempt to conceal her smile before standing up, with the pretense of leaving.

"I have no time —"

Antonio took her hand and kissed it. *"Time does not exist."*

"Dishes and clothes mending do. And I daresay you will once again remember time when it is time for supper."

"Hand me that piece of parchment, will you?"

"You have two hands and an able body. I am no servant to you or any other!"

His lips reached for her forehead, as he amusingly pulled her obstinacy towards him.

She looked away with a halfhearted reproach.

"You could always attend to the kitchen instead," he replied, his eyes dancing.

In an attempt to afflict bodily damage upon her opponent, Patria tickled him ruthlessly, sending him sprawling onto the floor.

They laughed, children caught in the moment.

"I cook for the love of it and the love of those I love,"

Patria scowled, reluctantly helping Antonio regain his former position.

"And I appreciate it more than you can imagine," Antonio smiled affectionately, as he reached out a hand to lightly stroke her tumbling tresses.

Patria pushed his hand away, but she was smiling again, this time without mockery or pretense.

There was silence for a moment. Patria hesitated, before recovering her former seat by Antonio. A warning glance wiped away his half-amused eyes of expectation.

Patria began to stroke the piano absentmindedly. Antonio smiled. He knew that she loved his music as much as he did himself.

"This may sound mad, but…I fell in love with you the first night you played for my father and myself. Here, with the familiar crackling of the cinders in the fire, you brought us to another place without allowing us to leave you. Through every note…I felt like…I grew to know you—know you very deeply."

"You were not the only one taken in at that moment."

"When the last note sounded—"

Now she reached for his hand.

"You were…are…what I heard. Every note…I…"

She broke herself off abruptly.

"If a meddling gossip heard me, I would soon be in the madhouse."

They both laughed.

Antonio shook his head. "Do not be ashamed of the greatest truth."

"I am not," she said defensively, yet softly, "I am simply accustomed to describing with my pen what I feel…in *secrecy. I feel so young, telling you these things."*

"So do I."

She smiled, and he held her close. When they finally moved apart, her eyes were misty with uncertain felicity.

"When shall we be wed?"

"Soon, I promise. In nearly a fortnight, I will have finished my apprenticeship. I will soon thereafter have a shop of my own. And, perhaps, one day, all that will be required for gold will be—"

"Your music," she finished, looking into his eyes.

*"Yes, **our** music."*

A loud clanging sound in the distance drew the two apart with a start.

Patria moved quickly, a grin alighting the corner of her lips.

"Ethel may require my assistance."

Only a few days earlier, the bumbling scullery maid had inadvertently allowed two pigeons meant for supper to exit through the kitchen window. Patria's father, the master of the house and the master of Antonio the Carpenter, was far from pleased.

He returned the knowing smile. "Until supper."

"Until supper."

His lips found hers, and he held her once more.

Another cacophonous warning cymbal drew Patria away. As she hurried for the nearest door, she found that she was not able to move very easily.

Their hands drew apart at the last moment in reluctant farewell.

They both grinned as Patria finally exited, the last note of the first movement.

Monet: Why is bread coming out of the piano?!
What is the meaning of this?!?!?!?

Morena: ¡Qué romántico!

Antonio: I actually am really impressed, Elise.
Bravo!

I paused before sending. For some reason, I felt a bit self-conscious sending romantic writings. Probably because he was a guy friend. And because this showed a side of me that...

I pressed "Send" and prayed that the email would be lost in cyberspace if it were not meant to be.

Chapter Twenty-Two

Deficit

It was Family Day.

And something was wrong.

"I'm just a little nervous," I told myself as I brushed back my hair. "After all, I've been planning this forever and I want it to be perfect. It's important to Peter. And…it's important to me."

I looked into the reflection of glass before me, two large, dark eyes staring back at me with worry.

My train of thought was severed as the flip-flop on my right foot caught on the alarm clock sitting on the bedroom floor. I fell, sprawling to the floor, with a yelp. It was then, when I eyed the mechanical culprit with distaste, that I noticed the time.

1:25 PM. I had to be there in five minutes. I jumped up quickly and began an urgent mission to find my necklace.

It was a song, a dance. The triumphant red, the immaculate white, and the gentle pink swirled together to form a maze of mazes, a hope of hopes.

The roses glided elegantly in the wind, unrestrained yet contained in baskets of dove's flight.

The procession.

The joy in my fellow parishioners' eyes, the intimate gesture of hand in hand—from large to small—caught me, and I was with them.

I led them. I stood before them, behind them, and beside them.

As we reached the parish hall, I recalled a moment from my childhood.

Dark brown fabric was held together by a simple band over his head. A flowing robe of the same color but a lighter hue was its counterpart. Beside him, dark brown locks peeked out from beneath pearly white; a bright, blue ribbon in her hair reflected the sash at her side. They squeezed the hand of a small child. **A small child.** *A vision of white and gold.*

The Holy Family.

It was St. Joseph's Day. Alexander was ten years old and I was eight. He took the part of Joseph and I played Mary. Between us was a small boy who had, two weeks earlier, eagerly announced his desire to play the most important role of all…the Christ child.

Little Alexander knocked on the door.

We stood before the parish hall. I raised my hand and knocked lightly on the door.

Peter answered.

And then I saw it.

He looked much the same; he stood, forever tall and confident, gentle yet firm. But something was different. Our eyes met for one, long moment. Then, with a single movement, he turned away swiftly as if nothing had transpired.

I suddenly fought the urge to cry and stared at myself in wonder. I blinked in confusion and led my group inside.

Four long tables were joined to form one in the center of the room. Several smaller tables were scattered across the perimeter of the room; they were booths set up for various family activities, from arts and crafts to family portraits. As I drew closer, I caught sight of Tom, who stood by the set of doors on the opposite end. He held up a large banner on which was written "Capture the Flag" in bold, red letters, and wore a large grin.

The single table of four was covered in white, and upon its surface was a splendid assortment of dishes. The luscious scent of many a delicacy, from roasted pork to pasta primavera, filled my senses with delight. Fluffy pastries and cookies of various shapes and sizes peeked out amongst loaves of freshly baked bread basking in small, closely woven baskets.

My stomach growled.

We gathered around the Table and joined hands. Father Muñoz stood on the opposite end, his robes purple with Lenten solemnity. He made the Sign of the Cross and bowed his head.

Our Father...

His deep voice was joined by dozens more.

Who art in Heaven
Hallowed be Thy Name
Thy kingdom come
Thy will be done
On Earth as it is in Heaven
Give us this day
Our daily bread
And forgive us our trespasses
As we forgive those who trespass against us
And lead us not into temptation
But deliver us from evil
Amen.

A moment of silence elapsed before Father Muñoz looked up and began to speak.

"I could say grace, but I think that today the honor lies with someone else," he said with a smile. "Will the person responsible for this ceremony step forward?"

I heard a slight rustling to my right and turned. Ten or so people away from me, Peter stood. An expression of contentment marked his countenance as he walked to stand next to the priest. As I looked at him, I almost forgot what had just transpired. He faced the crowd, his eyes a mixture of solemnity and peace. A quiet smile formed as he began to speak.

"Fellow parishioners, it is with great pleasure that I

share this occasion with you. It is one that is personally significant to me." Peter's voice grew softer. "It is one that we celebrate in my own country, Canada. In my home of Alberta."

Peter bent his head, closing his eyes.

Bless us O Lord
And these Thy gifts.
Which we are about to receive.

The waves of the sea tiptoed forward and then glided triumphantly as each voice joined his.

Many voices, yet one.

From Thy bounty, through Christ
Our Lord
Amen.

"Rebecca?"

I was kneeling beside a little girl who had, a few minutes earlier, eagerly tapped my shoulder to request assistance with her water color painting. It was of a small wooly lamb that lay by a wooden cross. At the sound of Peter's voice, I gently lay my hand on the child's shoulder and whispered that I would soon return. She nodded, golden curls beaming in their flight, as she continued her drawing, absolutely absorbed.

I stood, and turned towards Peter.

His eyes once again held me before his voice. Yet there was something about them that was detached from the Peter that I knew.

"Would you mind taking over the family photo booth for a bit?" he asked, his voice calm and even.

"Sure. No problem," I quickly replied.

I turned away before he could see the question in my eyes, and began to walk with as much purpose as I could assume. Even then, without seeing, I felt his eyes follow me as I left.

Two delightful beach balls of vibrant colors bounced up and down excitedly about a large net held together by two silver poles.

A family of four.

I smiled, indicating with my hand where they should stand along the box of dotted lines marked on the floor. I observed the scene, changing the angle and making suggestions until I saw the picture that this family deserved.

Photography had been a passion of mine since childhood. For an instant, my mind held nothing else as I remained completely mesmerized by the art, which was a painting and, subsequently, a story.

Yet, as the camera clicked with timely precision, I caught, out of the corner of my eye, a glimpse of Peter. He knelt beneath an arch of roses, and his face was in his hands.

Chapter Twenty-Three

Visus

Family Day was, by and large, a success. At the end of the celebration, Peter and I had stood at the door, offering pamphlets of cultural information regarding the origin of the holiday. It seemed that praise was never-ending as smiling and laughing families exited the parish hall.

But, in the rush of things, I had not had time to ask Peter what was wrong. I had not had time to decipher the mystery of Peter's sad eyes.

He seemed his usual self as we stood by that door, calm and collected. I thought for a moment that I had imagined it all or, at least, the extent of his misery.

Perhaps he was just worried about finals, which, for him, were the first three days of the following week. Yet, every once in a while, I caught his eye's truth for a single instant.

No, it wasn't just the anxiety brought on by the thought of upcoming finals. It was something much, much deeper.

I thought briefly of asking him in our next *Intermission* correspondence, but quickly dismissed the idea. It just wouldn't seem...right. I had to ask in person.

lighthousekeeper45@yahoo.com writes:

```
~Monet's Version~
     Enjoy! :)
```

"Antonio!" Patrie smiled at her darling sweetly. "You need to stop this pianist nonsense and entertain higher pursuits...such as cooking, for example. I hear that the French cuisine is superior in all ways."

Antonio: He is a musician! A musician for life! And he doesn't want to be a cook!

Elise: If **Antonio** says that he's a musician for life, then he's a musician for life!

Antonio: And her name is Patria! It's Italian, not French!

Elise: Oh, I'm *so* glad you liked the name Patria, **Antonio**!

Antonio: I didn't…say that.

Morena: Interesting twist…

It was Wednesday. I pressed "Send."
Three days later, I still had not heard from him.
It was not like him.
Surely he was still recovering from finals, I reasoned. Surely he was too wiped out to respond.
Surely.

Chapter Twenty-Four

Tactus

"We give You our 'what ifs', 'yes, but's', and 'could be's', our confusion and hopes. May our prayers be answered in the timing, manner, and intensity that You choose."

Amen.

It was the sixth Sunday of Lent. *Palm Sunday.*

Peter wasn't here.

Tom had collected our baskets during the Presentation of the Gifts. I watched his retreating figure with confusion and then turned slightly to scan the rows of parishioners as far as my eye could see.

Perhaps he had served at an earlier Mass. Perhaps

he was here. Yet my heart told me that he had not, and was not.

I gazed at the Crucifix before me. My eyes grasped hold of something that they had somehow missed before…through all the years that I had attended Mass at St. Vitus'. Perhaps I had seen it before, but not *truly* seen.

Or perhaps it was now that I was *called* to see it.

On the Cross, the Beloved Son lay, arms outstretched, embracing humanity. *The Sacrifice, a Sacrifice of Love.* Yet behind that image were two images more, two gently-shaded shadows. The image closest to the Cross was of a lighter tone, almost fading away into the immaculate white of the wall; the other was slightly darker. And, together, the two soft forms, overlapping yet distinct, were like misty wings of silence, exquisitely-spun and spread full, surrounding our Lord in graceful symphony.

They were more than shadows cast by the figure on a wooden cross. They were His angels.

And the two sets of heavenly wings surrounded a three-fold image that remained One.

I held three palms in my hand. My skin was still slightly bathed in coolness, the coolness of the holy water that Father Muñoz had sprinkled as he walked down the aisle, large branches of green in hand, from row to row.

I would bring them to the Cross.

As I genuflected, exiting the pew, I was overcome by a curious feeling. I knew the reason, yet I failed to understand. I walked, drawn by custom to the small room at the back of the church. *To the usher's closet.*

In the space before the door so often occupied by Peter stood a new figure.

It was Cedric.

Wisps of white and gray assembled themselves atop a dignified surface. They swirled, turning and mixing into great, circular whirlpools below. I had seen him often in the distance, his pensive yet amused eyes like dancing sentinels. Yet I had never before seen the conical straw hat dangling precariously in soft, invisible lines above his head.

The parrot, all bright feathers of blue, red, and green, joyfully caressed his rosy cheeks.

He was Fred. How had I failed to see it before?

I took a step backward in surprise.

And, now that I could see what I had not seen before, but had always been present, I was able to see something new.

The usual mirth displayed on his countenance remained, but a portion of it was withdrawn into the halls of memory. A line of worry creased his brow.

Then, in that moment, sentinel, hat, and parrot, together, caught sight of me.

Cedric smiled quietly, instantly raising his great eyes to study my face. "Rebecca, isn't it?"

"Yes," I smiled back. "I think I heard Peter call you Cedric?"

He nodded and said nothing, standing, waiting.

He knew. There was no need for small talk. And, as I opened my mouth to ask the question, the answer had already resounded in my mind.

"Is Peter here?"

"No," he paused, "he had to leave for Canada."

Despite my 'premonitions', I almost took another step backwards.

Peter had left the country...and without telling me? I stared in confusion. That didn't sound like him. And he...*had* to?

"Why?" I asked blankly.

The old man stood there in silence. It was obvious that, if he knew anything (and I was pretty sure that he did), he wasn't going to tell me.

My face suddenly burned in anger. *I'm Peter's friend*, I wanted to yell. *I have the right to know what is going on.* I *had* to know if everything was okay.

But then I remembered Fred, and saw that Cedric's large, dark eyes spoke to me with something akin to sympathy. My forehead cooled.

There was nothing more that I could say.

I looked down at my feet. "I'd better get going. Thanks for letting me know."

Cedric nodded slowly, his eyes still holding my gaze, penetrating, yet compassionate. They were searching my own, searching to make sure that I was all right.

I wasn't, not really. But I didn't know enough to really worry.

Right?

Then why was I worried?

I attempted to shake off these persistent feelings, leaning over slightly to pick up a copy of the weekly bulletin, my face composed.

"Have a good day," I said. I readjusted my purse strap and began to head for the door.

"Rebecca."

I turned.

His misty gray eyes had grown stronger, as if illuminated by some unseen candle.

"He cares about you."

I looked back at him, a snapshot of myself reflected in his eyes. "I know."

The door closed soundlessly behind me. I began to walk in the shadows of a deliberate march, making my way towards the car, pretending that nothing significant had transpired.

Had it?

"Hi, Rebecca!"

I turned swiftly to meet the large, brown eyes of Father D'Angelo.

"Hey, Father!" I smiled quickly.

Too quickly. It was forced.

And he saw that...saw that as his eyes met mine once again, his mouth filled with anticipated words that were quickly tossed aside far beyond his enveloping robes. He opened and then closed his mouth, looking at me in silence for several moments.

He finally reached into a small bag that he was

carrying. I stood, waiting, as his hand searched inside the bag. It finally caught hold of something, and this he held up.

It was a rose. Around and around, the mystical web was spun. But it was not an ordinary rose—if any rose may be called ordinary—not one sprung from a garden. As I inspected it more closely, I realized that the rose petals were composed of delicate lines of green. *A palm rose.* A maze of palms.

Father D'Angelo held it out to me. I mumbled a polite "thank you," shuffling my feet in confusion.

Confusion brought by understanding. Understanding that I did not know how to comprehend.

"There is something special about a palm woven into a rose." His eyes met mine, quiet and understanding, filled with the wisdom of the ages.

I nodded.

He briefly touched my shoulder, a firm grasp that seemed somehow to impart strength. "Keep it."

"I will, Father."

I opened my closet, looking for something to wear. We would soon leave for Grandma and Grandpa's house.

I had changed to my pajamas. This wasn't unusual; I sometimes did this even when there was a short intermission between one activity and the next. But, for some reason, I had really needed to feel comfortable.

I spotted the pink, flowered blouse that I had worn

when Peter had come over to visit only a few weeks earlier. *When he bent before our tortoise, inspecting her closely. When we swung high into the sky, laughing, free from all worry, all problems. When we sat quietly in thought, loud in inspiration, looking at our story together.*

"Rebecca!"

I nearly jumped at the sound of my father's voice calling in the distance. I had been staring at the contents of my closet, forgetting that I was supposed to select something. I rushed to my bed, putting on the clothes that I had worn to church earlier.

I heard the blaring sound of the TV as I walked down the hall. When I reached the family room, I noticed that the news station was on. *Breaking News* flashed at the bottom of the screen.

"That's horrible!" my dad sighed, pointing to the television set. "A plane crash…there have been too many of those lately."

I read the headline just as the newscaster echoed what I saw.

The destination of the plane had been Alberta, Canada.

Right, back, down, up, and over. Square. Front, right, pull.

I finished my seventh palm cross. Once you started, it was hard to stop. Grandma Allegretti looked up and smiled from the adjacent sofa. She was probably on her tenth. This was something that we had done together since I was on about the seventh—or tenth—year of my life. She had taught me, and I had learned. Sometimes I would think that I had forgotten how as a new spring approached. But it soon came back as I watched my grandma's long, tapered fingers move through the familiar pattern, to magically reveal her product in what seemed like the blink of an eye.

And these simple, yet complex, movements were soothing.

"Rebecca dear, could you get the door? It must be your grandpa with the pie."

I jumped up, but Alexander was already walking towards the door. I sat down again, and concentrated on making my eighth cross.

Ninth.

Tenth.

Then I got up from the sofa, lightly touching Grandma's shoulder as I left the room in search of Grandpa.

I strongly believed in being honest about your feelings.

But I had to hide it.

My grandparents didn't need the stress.

And it was Palm Sunday.

It was a joyous occasion. Jesus had entered Jerusalem to the triumphant cries of a crowd shouting *Hosanna* and waving palm branches.

I couldn't ruin that.

I didn't have the *right* to ruin that.

I walked down the hall. And, as I did, an image from home formed in my mind.

It is on the mantel, to the right of the soft sculpture

of the Virgin Mary and Baby Jesus.

An array of color meets the eye; the deep crimson of wine solidifies, swirls into the lines and curves of its brother, a vibrant tie of red and green. The owner of the tie, a young boy, stands behind the chair of an older woman with dark brown hair and broad-rimmed glasses. Dressed elegantly in white, she is turned slightly towards him, a smile illuminating her face. To the left of the boy stands a young girl, a few years younger than he. A floral wreath of snow is the counterpart to her gown of white. It was her First Communion dress, but is now used for another occasion. And, to her left, seated beside the woman of the silver spectacles is an elderly man dressed in formal attire of black and white. With large, dark eyes, he gazes intently at the camera. It is a look that speaks of the centuries…

This was my favorite photograph of all time, taken at my grandparents' fiftieth anniversary party. It drew the eye, it drew *my* eye, because of its artistic portrayal of a beautiful Truth of which I was a part. Each and every angle seemed perfect…from Grandma turning lovingly toward her grandson to the blissful expression on my countenance as my eyes, almost closed, almost cast downward, remain directed toward my grandfather with a sort of inner peace. Each angle was an embrace.

It was a snapshot of True Love.

Yet, in this picture, what struck me as most remarkable was the expression on my grandfather's face. In that gaze, you saw the poet, the WWII veteran, the 'retired' psychologist still called upon from time to time for advice—the psychologist that inspired me to choose that profession—and, above all, my grandpa.

Knowledge formed in the recesses of my mind that was confirmed as I descended the short steps to the library.

This is never going to get past Grandpa.

He was sitting, on a softly colored sofa of earth tones, relaxed, yet tired, as he was recuperating from a cold.

I smiled and bent down to give him a kiss.

He looked at me.

"Let's take a walk."

He relinquished his seat on the sofa, asking Alexander to join us.

He didn't ask what was on my mind. But I followed.

I opened the latch to the backyard.

My grandparents' garden was something that had been with me my entire life.

Grandpa gave us a tour, enumerating the latest additions such as the pumpkins that a priest-friend had planted, as well as remarking upon the usual inhabitants of the place.

It was cool with a slight breeze.

Thyme, basil, mint, rosemary, arugula…Grandpa took a few leaves of each, handing them to two small children who eagerly scrunched the scented green and held it closer to their faces.

We continued walking, as a different area of the garden called to us.

We were kneading the dough for challah, a Jewish

tradition adopted in a Jesuit bread-baking book given by my Irish father to my Italian grandfather.

Farther.

Grandpa was mixing jams again, to Grandma's horror.

I leaned over for a glimpse of any remaining pumpkins.

I sat at my grandfather's desk, in the library once again. Before me was a list of poems from different volumes of his poetry. He had selected some in particular with publication in mind.

The tomato plants awaited us.

An enthusiastic ten-year-old with brown, curly hair placed a finger on the "Record" button of a cassette tape player. Grandpa's thoughtful voice recounted the days of the Battle of the Bulge.

We went back inside.

And then the mango tree called.

With a fruit picker, a basket, and some bags in hand, we headed over to the front yard to take hold of the luscious ruby delight that awaited us.

I reached for the nearest branch. I reached higher.

And I found, as I dodged branches, brushing locks of hair from my face, twisted a stem in order to release the fruit, and, finally, placed the product delicately into a basket, that I gained strength.

My grandpa was sitting on the planter, watching my brother and me at work, thoughtful, smiling.

And, somewhere, between the picking of this mango and the placing of the next in the basket on the ground, a true smile, a true laugh, broke through the sense of foreboding that had been present, deep within my chest, from the instant that I saw the headline.

I think Grandpa saw that.

And, as we faced the task, the journey, before us, a familiar figure appeared, walking slowly, with a slight limp, from the house to the left of us. It was Cordelia, my grandparents' neighbor of forty years. Her twin sister had died a few months earlier, and her eldest grandson, a soldier in the Marines, was missing.

My heart instantly turned towards her. As one, we left the mango tree and met her.

The cost of college.

Easter.

Her children…home for the holidays.

Much was said.

But what stood out in our conversation the most was her answer to a question that had never been asked.

"What are you doing for Easter?" I asked gently.

"I'm doing okay," she said.

*She had heard, "How are **you** doing?" Yet I realized that that was what I had really meant.*

Cordelia continued, "We were more than just twins by blood. We were so much alike. I remember this time," she smiled in recollection, "when we were little and tried to find a treasure chest in our backyard. We were convinced that it existed, in our backyard of all backyards. After weeks of searching, we finally found it. I didn't find out until later that Dad had felt sorry for us and planted it there a few days before."

Cordelia and Grandpa chuckled together.

I looked at them and recalled.

"Treasure comes in many different forms," Grandpa said softly.

Cordelia nodded, a wistful smile filling her countenance.

"And, when you love someone, there is always hope…hope in one form or another. And, when there is loss, you never lose because any Light truly ingrained in your heart will always be with you."

Grandpa was speaking of Anthony, Cordelia's grandson, and of Cynthia, her sister. But he was also speaking to me, to Alexander, to all of us.

Cordelia gave my brother and me each a hug before she left. When she asked if we were doing well, I wondered if she saw something.

My thoughts wandered.

But the mango tree called.

As I reached for a branch, I saw my father exit the house and walk towards us. My brother had given me the picker this time. I wasn't quite sure how this was going to go.

My dad's strong arms reached mine as we, together, pulled the mangoes from their old home. I felt like a little girl again.

True Love.

I turned on my back.

I couldn't sleep.

And it was unlikely that I would fall asleep on my back, I reminded myself. I still would fall asleep on my stomach, just as I had when I was a little girl.

Some things never changed.

I sighed, propping my head up with one hand. I wished that the tranquility that had finally settled in the late afternoon were with me now. Sometimes life is like that, I thought. A fleeting moment of bliss filling your existence with ecstasy, only to fade with the dimming light.

No, I could not believe that.

But I was caught in an hourglass of colliding dreams.

And, as I shifted between different positions, over and over again, a thought that I couldn't ignore came to surface.

I was scared. I was scared for Peter.

It didn't matter whether it was unlikely that he had stepped on that plane of all planes, on this day of all days. It wouldn't matter until I knew with certainty that he was okay.

I pursed my lips together and gazed up at the ceiling.

And I suddenly came to understand that the thought of Peter leaving my life, as quickly and unexpectedly as he had entered it, killed me. He couldn't. He just couldn't.

A familiar image crossed my mind, an image of great azure waves breathing, echoing, under the moving arms of a gentle sea breeze. And light…light burst forth over the entire surface in a dance that became a song, a song without words. A song that could be heard only if you listened very, very closely.

A tapestry of Light.

Peter was a part of this, and so great a part of it that few had and few would ever be able to occupy in my life.

He was a part of the Everything that I knew.

I squeezed my eyes shut—my eyes, burning, torched—and opened my heart to the Greatest Eternity.

God, please don't take away my angel. Please.

Déjà vu.

I was there.

I heard the waves tumbling in a chorus of doves, inviting me to take part in their vision. A vision from Beyond.

I breathed it in.

My feet traced the intersection of tiny prints.

I was present.

Baila.

My lungs filled with words, dreams.

Whole Dreams.

That was…beautiful.

They swirled about me, held me, kept me by the sand-scattered shore.

Coincidence.

I moved to the side, shadows playing catch and seek on unseen walls.

On the contrary, everyone is here.

The fleeting moment became Whole.

As I walked to the dining room table, a bundle of palm crosses on the mantel, lying in rest by an emerald rose, caught my eye.

I took one in my hand, staring at it for a few moments.

I would give it to Peter when I saw him next.

With the palm in hand, I took a seat at the table. Unknown words spoke to me. I picked up my pen. *A pen of an intricate floral design. The pen that Peter had given to me.*

And, then—

It nudged its way forward, tiptoeing until it grew louder, more distinct.

It came to me.

And I smiled.

Chapter Twenty-Five

Gustus

scrambled
        understanding
    Forgotten
        Truth

A circular form, a cross engraved. A chalice, holding, full.

I faced the Blessed Sacrament in the Adoration Chapel.

I felt a prayer.

I was alone, except for a short woman with thick, red hair a few pews over. She sat, her hands joined, her face in her hands.

Her face in her hands. Like Peter on Family Day.

I had emailed Peter, asking if he was okay. I had explained that I had heard about the plane crash.

I had waited. As yet, there was no reply.

And I had never thought to ask for his phone number.

Brilliant.

I closed my eyes.

Life wouldn't mean much if it were just a random array of happenings, a mix and match of coincidences. But it was this meaning that could hurt...could make you hurt so much.

Yet it was still worth it.

As she bent in prayer, wide sleeves of a faint flower print brushed against her hands, long fingers against a silver circlet around her ring finger.

Half of a memory surfaced in my mind.

What was it?

I was not alone.

Yes.

Adoro Te Devote.

I heard a slight rustling to my right as the woman of flowers arose from her seat to make a quiet exit.

God, please keep Peter safe. Please keep him well. I care, I care so much. Help him, my dear Lord. Help me. I put our lives in Your hands.

Amen.

I arose, stopping to genuflect before leaving the aisle. As I reached the door, I turned back for an instant, my eyes once again drawn to the Blessed

Sacrament.

A circular form, holy and true. A circular form within a monstrance. Within a golden monstrance.

Half a memory that never was surfaced.

What was it?

Don't try so hard, boy. Feel your way around it.

A lighthouse. A lighthouse and a portal to the sea.

A sea of Intermission.

It was then that I knew.

I closed the chapel door behind me.

Far ahead, in front of the church, the dark silhouette of a tall figure rose against the colors of the painted night sky.

I impulsively ran to it, chasing the image before it would disappear, pulling a golden piece of paper from my purse, half afraid that it would likewise vanish.

I had known somehow that he would be there, just as he knew that I would come.

I caught my breath, standing in silence before the now distinct figure, caught in wonder.

I held out the paper containing the word "Intermission," tears in my eyes. "You wrote this, didn't you?"

"Yes," Cedric said, a quiet smile inching its way across his face, "yes, I did."

I stared absentmindedly at the computer screen.

He had told me little. He had told me little and I had asked for little more. I had opened my mouth dozens of times, overcome by dozens of words echoing "why" and "how," only to close it once more.

Somewhere beneath my innate curiosity and ever-active detective mind was a realization that the mystery was enough.

No, not enough. *More than enough.*

And he wouldn't have told me anyway.

I heaved a sigh, a sigh of both satisfaction and puzzlement.

But...who was he?

What was he?

Another lost memory surfaced, filling my being with quiet serenity.

He was Fred.

He was the sea captain.

I shook my head, smiling.

And that was enough.

Sky became water; water, sky. The glassy surface of an iridescent lake became a mirror, a mirror that reflected the brilliant azure of the heavens above. Deep green pine trees shot to the heavens, guarding this world of glass and stone, sentinels growing taller and taller along the lightly trodden

path. Dark grey figures splashed with the whitest paint became mountain kings watching their kingdoms from afar. This was not a just a place; it was a world.

No wonder Peter loves it so much, I thought, as I gazed in wonder at the picturesque sight before me made possible by a Google Image search. *How beautiful.*

And, as I looked through these pictures, reluctantly moving to the next, wishing to never leave the sight of one, I came to understand Peter, the boy that I knew, even more.

Welcome to Alberta, Wild Rose Country.

It was a sign, complete with the dainty picture of a pink rose. I closed my eyes, remembering. *Alberta, known for the rose. And a battered old notebook. A battered old notebook with a familiar poem affixed to its cover.* A deep sigh arose from the depths of my heart.

 Winter

  Spring

 Autumn

   Summer

 picture

  after

   picture

 Each so exquisite

  Each so unique.

I hope you are there now, Peter. In this beautiful world of yours.

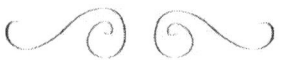

Monday

nothing

Do not ignore this one fact, beloved,

Tuesday

nada

nada

that with the Lord one day is like a
thousand years...

I turned to Chelsey as Dr. Everson passed out
the testing booklets. "Good luck, Chelsey."

She looked up with a smile from the seat next to
me. "Good luck to you, too!"

and a thousand years like one day.

Wednesday

No word yet, Adriana.

The Lord does not delay his promise,
as some regard
    "delay,"

```
but he is patient with you,
      not wishing that any should perish
```

I turned off the CD player.
I was lost in a world of words.
A poem lay on my desk. I caught it.

```
      but   that   all   should   come   to
repentance.
            2 Peter 3:8-9
```

Thursday

"Good luck, guys."
Sheets of paper, stapled neatly in the
      top
left hand
corner
      appeared before my eyes.
The physics test.
Formulas, and hypotheses, and mathematical
functions rolled around
        in my head
          doing work
          using energy
As I began to pick up my pencil, a flash of silver
caught my eye. It was a necklace, a simple chain
holding the delicate form of a smooth seashell.

Full of Light.

I remembered.

`Heavenly Father, guide Rebecca...your`
`servant, Peter.`

My heart dove, and rolled, and

smiled.

I picked up my newly-sharpened pencil and began the test.

I jumped at the sound of the doorbell. I was sitting at the kitchen table, relaxed, "Only the Beginning Of The Adventure" playing softly in the background.

Dad.

His eyes.

I moved forward.

The snow, white and immaculate, tiptoed, drew closer. It was the wing of a gentle dove, gliding gracefully in flight, a dove of many. It became more distinct, closer, closer. Hundreds of priests donned in white solemnly stepped forward. One of them was Father D'Angelo, his merry eyes now quiet, now sad, yet peaceful.

Many friends. One in their Love.

For God.

And for His servants.

For Monsignor McGregor.

The passing of an angel.

My eyes grew moist. I turned to my dad, who stood on my left, his eyes glazed, his face drawn into an expressionless sadness.

The first notes of a song, both life-giving and scorching, beautiful and heart-wrenching, were called forth.

I took his hand, and raised it high above to the mango tree.

*Lo inmortal *

Las hojas pintadas de rojo vuelan
Sin moverse de su santuario.
Un paso las marca por muerte
Y quedan inmaculadas sin arruga.
Llaman al viento del viejo ayer
Pero siempre están en el presente
Y sin duda quedan inscritas
En la larga noche del futuro.
El color brillante sonríe
Con la suave sutileza del amanecer
Un nuevo comienzo que ya había nacido
Hace una indeleble eternidad.

Ninguna hoja es idéntica
No conoce el mismo tono.
El rojo de alba
Y el rojo de crepúsculo

I Thirst

La llegada y la salida.
Como sus compañeros del libro
Uno nunca parece como el anterior
Pero conoce el mismo aire.
Hay tantas hojas que vuelan
Sin moverse de su santuario.

Y el vuelo continúa sin empezar.

* See Appendix for translation.

Chapter Twenty-Six

In

It was Good Friday.

I sat in a pew on the left side of the church, towards the middle.

Away with him! Away with him! Crucify him! Crucify him!

Roman guards towered over the drably-dressed crowd, imposing in their long, deep red robes. A few moments earlier, they had been laughing teenagers awaiting the dawn of a relaxing vacation.

Except Bob. Bob had once again been cast as the eldest of the Roman guards. His eyes met mine for an instant before he quickly turned away.

Peter was not there.

The congregation sat in quiet reverence, drawn in, further, further, waiting.

The ringing of a march collided with the softly pulsing air.

A young man, portraying Jesus of Nazareth, walked down the center aisle
     no, down the path
       of the Place of the
         Skull
He held a wooden cross before him
      the guard's whip cracking at his heels.
As he continued, he began to stumble.
     The blow fell harder.
      The whip, a piercing blade, accosted his back, scorched his arms, maligned his side.
     No, never maligned.
     They could not soil the pure, cast out the holy.
     But they tried.
     And He let them
     He let them for us.

He drew closer to the altar. *An altar of today, a church timeless*
     Of centuries later, of today, tomorrow, and yesterday.
     And then I saw it.
     Overlapping glimmers of wings
     Wings trembling
     A trembling angel
     Two images, overlapping,
       One taller, larger, greater,

an encompassing image of the All.

A crown of thorns.

I thirst.

And, another, smaller with

overlapping shadows of wings

wings trembling

struggling, falling

bent in

Pain.

I rushed forward, holding out my arms,

closer, closer

reaching, hands outstretched.

My heart swelled as I leaned towards the bent figure, my entire being caught up in the necessity to grasp one of the silent wings, barely distinguishable in the faint light.

Falling, falling

Two images overlapping

No, I will carry your cross.

I rushed forward and cradled his limp form.

I touched a glimpse.

The wing drew about me.

I knelt, unable to move.

It lifted, as if an eye cast upward, and I followed it.

A crack of lightning sounded.

The outline of the larger figure that I had seen before grew larger, became filled with a brilliant

LIGHT

I bent in awe.

I

The winged figure and I

We dropped to our knees, although we were already kneeling.

I closed my eyes, and, when I opened them, after minutes or, perhaps, hours, I could just barely make out one set of wings, vibrating out of focus, growing softer, dimmer, less distinct...

I was sitting in the pew once again.

And, with dozens more, I gazed at a single figure on a wooden cross.

And Peter.

Peter and me at the foot of the Cross.

SCENE 15

In a Banquet Hall:

The four friends, Monet, Antonio, Elise, and Morena, gather to celebrate prior to the first performance of their play, an adaptation of the original lighthouse story. Word of the unique jam shop troupe had reached many across the country, who are now gathered to enjoy the entertainment provided. Tickets for the opening night are also available at this event, sold by Fred of Duku jam fame, who volunteered to assist. Monet and Antonio strike up a conversation as they sip some root beer; Morena and Elise sit in the audience, enjoying the music of the band hired for the night.

Antonio [sipping his drink]: Well, my friend, I have to admit…you were right. It WAS meant to be a play.

Monet [smiles smugly, although, this time, it is mostly put on]: Of course I was.

[The two laugh heartily. **Elise** turns at the sound and waves at **Antonio** with a smile. The two men observe.]

Antonio: At least she didn't blow me a kiss.

Monet: Silly girl. Almost as silly as you are.

[**Antonio** glares at **Monet**, who laughs and heartily slaps him on the back. **Antonio** coughs for a moment at the force of the impact.]

Monet [clears throat]: The girl may be silly and sentimental, but she has a good heart. And, despite my elevated tastes, I do agree with you that her writing, while leaving something to be desired, is decent for her age.

Antonio [thoughtfully]: That scene with Antonio and Patria *was* beautiful.

Monet [grins]: *Antonio* and Patria. And who do you

suppose Patria was supposed to be?

Antonio [groans]: I should have known.

[**Elise** relinquishes her seat and walks up to **Antonio**.]

Elise [smiles sweetly]: You owe me a dance tonight, Mr. Martinelli.

Antonio [smiles innocently]: I have the perfect number picked out.

Elise [blushes]: Oh! What is it?

Antonio [offhandedly]: Oh, a traditional song for the tarantella.

Elise [blinks]: Tarantella? What does that mean?

Antonio [smiles widely]: An Italian word for…tarantula.

[Several members of the audience turn as **Elise** runs back to her seat, shrieking. **Antonio** adjusts his tie with a self-assured smile.]

Monet [laughs; slaps **Antonio** on the back again, initiating another coughing fit]: In all seriousness, have you ever thought that maybe you should consider Elise?

Antonio [recovering from coughing fit]: Elise? Are you mad?! That girl has been chasing me for years. And she *is* silly…a silly and frivolous twit. Didn't you just see her?!

Monet [grins]: All those who are in love may appear to be quite silly.

[**Antonio** looks at **Elise**, who, having recovered, is now attentively watching the musicians play with a peaceful countenance.]

Antonio [thoughtfully]: She really loves music, doesn't she?

Monet [nods, trying not to laugh]: Just like you.

Antonio: And…she's rather pretty, don't you think?

Monet [hides his mouth in his hands with a snort]: Unquestionably.

Antonio: And an impressive writer.

Monet: Better than some.

[**Antonio** turns back at **Monet**, who has begun to chuckle unmercifully.]

Antonio [glares]: You tried to trick me!

Monet [eyes widen innocently]: I just want what is
    best for my two friends.

Antonio: Scoundrel!

Monet: Infidel!

[The two draw imaginary swords from the air and
begin to mock-fight. **Elise** turns around just as
Monet "stabs" **Antonio** in the stomach. He falls
dramatically to the floor. She taps **Morena** on the
shoulder, who joins her observations.]

Morena [laughs]: Some things never change.

Elise [also laughing]: I guess not.

[**Antonio** arises from the floor, brushing off his
pants with a sniff. **Monet** surveys him with a smile
of superiority.]

Antonio [glares]: Cheater!

Monet: We shall see tomorrow at 2:45!

Antonio: Usual place?

Monet: Naturally. I do not wish to allow you any
    particular advantage due to more pleasant

circumstances. We meet by the bee tree!

Antonio [heartily]: Agreed!

[The two shake hands on it and turn around to observe the band for a few minutes as it picks up a vibrant salsa beat. **Elise** whispers something in **Morena**'s ear, who smiles and nods. She leaves her seat to join **Monet** and **Antonio**.]

Elise [smiles sweetly at **Antonio**]: This is a great song!

Antonio [shrugs casually]: It's all right, I suppose.

Elise [enthusiastically]: A great song for *dancing*!

Antonio [shrugs again]: So I've heard.

Elise [exasperated]: Would you like to dance with me?

Antonio [flatly]: No.

[**Elise** glares at **Antonio** and then **Monet**, who is trying yet again not to laugh. She flounces off to her seat in a huff.]

Monet [sighs dramatically]: Antonio, Antonio, if you change your mind belatedly, it may be too late. This is the first time I've actually seen the girl frustrated by your usual attempts to dissuade her.

Antonio [shrugs]: Maybe she'll learn her lesson.

[**Monet** crosses his arms and looks at **Antonio** cross-eyed.]

Antonio [irritably]: FINE! I will *consider* it. *Consider*.

Monet [smiles]: Perhaps you're not such an imbecile after all.

[**Monet** lifts his hand to slap **Antonio** on the back again. **Antonio** moves away in horror.]

Antonio: Uh, yes, but no, uh, need for that.

Monet [moves hand back sheepishly]: Sorry.

[The band completes its last song. A middle-aged woman announces the next in the line-up, a young violinist from France, an addition made possible by **Monet**.]

Monet [watching]: If you didn't just play serious violin music, you could be up there.

Antonio [glares]: It is not serious. It is…art!

Monet [laughs heartily]: Let the violin become a

fiddle, boy. Or would that be too much of a challenge for you?

Antonio [glares]: *Nothing* is too great a challenge for Antonio Martinelli! And there may be times when a violin must...become a fiddle!

[**Antonio** marches purposefully towards the stage as **Monet** observes with an expression of mingled amusement and exasperation. **Elise** watches, her eyes all stars and roses, and **Morena** shakes her head with a smile. **Antonio** grabs the violin from the surprised musician just as he makes his way to the stage. He shoos him away. The announcer protests, but, with one look at **Antonio**, he retreats and the young violinist mutters something incoherent and leaves the stage with his apologies. **Antonio** approaches the microphone confidently.]

Antonio [smugly]: Sorry, there has been a slight change in plans. Welcome Antonio the Magnificent!

[Cheers are heard from the audience, **Elise**'s clapping and screams the loudest of all. **Monet** shakes his head and attempts to catch the French violinist before he leaves, to no avail. With an uncharacteristically casual shrug, he joins the audience, sitting in the empty seat next to **Morena**. **Antonio** begins to play a lively folk tune. The audience applauds wildly and some get up to dance.]

Elise [fans herself]: Isn't he just *wonderful*?!

[**Elise** suddenly relinquishes her seat and runs up to the stage. She throws her arms around **Antonio**, kissing him. At first, **Antonio** resists, but he finally gives in, pulling her closer. **Morena** and **Monet** exchange looks and begin to laugh. **Antonio** finally pulls away from **Elise**, blushing.]

Antonio [stammers]: Uh, slight detour. I will now continue.

Elise [screams]: Let's hear it for Antonio the Magnificent!

[The roar of the crowd becomes deafening. **Antonio** turns to **Elise** with an appreciative smile. She grins from ear to ear, and he begins the next song, which is as vibrant as the first. **Monet** stands, and turns to **Morena** with a bow.]

Monet: May I have the honor of this dance, my friend?

Morena [laughs]: Why not?

[The two friends begin to spin around quickly to the beat of the music, laughing all the way. **Elise** attempts to kiss **Antonio** again, as he plays on. **Fred** observes the four from the ticket booth and smiles.]

Chapter Twenty-Seven

Te

I looked up at the Crucifix and smiled.

Peter was alive.

He had arrived on the 4:30 AM plane earlier that morning. Cedric had informed me when I stepped into St. Vitus' to pray. Relief washed over me. I was able to breathe again and, now that I could, I was bombarding Cedric with questions.

Where is he now? I had asked impatiently, excitement filling me with sweet delight. *I need to talk to him.*

Cedric had shaken his head, smiling. "He said that you might ask about him...said also that you could find him after religious education classes in the church school today around 2:45 PM."

Okay, I could wait that long. I grasped the old man's hand gratefully. "Thank you."

He nodded, smiling.

Yet, as I walked away, I saw, out of the corner of my eye, a concerned expression in Cedric's great eyes.

And I did not know what that meant.

My Lord, thank you so much for bringing Peter safely home. And...please guide everything concerning him. I feel, deep in my heart, that there is something else—"

I heard the sound of a familiar someone clearing her throat, and turned around.

Adriana stood awkwardly to the left of my pew, as if uncertain how to proceed.

"Sorry for interrupting." Her eyes met mine apologetically.

I waved my hand. "No apology necessary. Join me?"

Adriana nodded, and I scooted slightly to the right. We sat there, lost in thought, found in prayer, a companionable silence touching our hearts.

Whether several seconds or several minutes, half an hour or two hours, passed, I would never know. I talked to God about many things during this time...Dad, school, Monsignor McGregor, Peter, prayers of which I had not been conscious before—all burst forth from my heart in one, single bound. I collected them, offering them to God. *To my Lord, Jesus Christ.*

Collected a rose, a palm, and a seashell.

As if planned by some unseen force, we finished praying at the same time, simultaneously touching our heads, chests, and shoulders in the Sign of the Cross. *In the Sign of His Cross.* We genuflected and moved into the aisle. I turned to leave, but Adriana caught me by the shoulder first.

Her eyes spoke bewilderment, pain, conflict.

"Can we stay with Him a bit longer?" she asked, pointing to the Cross.

Concern washed over me. *What was wrong?* But I knew Adriana; it would come out when she was ready to speak.

I nodded and followed her back to our previously occupied pew.

The three of us sat together for several minutes, waiting, *being*.

Adriana finally spoke, "Sometimes I just like to sit here and take in the immensity of God. In the silence of the church…or the Adoration Chapel."

I nodded, understanding. *What a paradox my best friend could be at times. Silent, Adriana? And yet it all seemed to make sense.*

She gazed far ahead, beyond us to the Beyond. "Have you ever felt like you were caught in a maze in which nothing made sense? In which you saw Superman and the Green Goblin in the same comic strip when they really belonged in two different stories?"

I nodded, thinking of Peter. "Yes."

"Kind of like…a forest."

My jaw dropped as familiarity sunk in.

But not reality…it was a dream…

A dream which had been reality all along.

"The forest!" I exclaimed.

"What?" Adriana eyed me curiously.

"Of all the stupidest clichés!" I groaned. I closed my eyes tightly and felt like screaming.

"You okay?" Adriana put her hand on my shoulder.

"Yeah. Sorta."

So, it had all been real. All true. The dream of the forest that I had experienced so long ago was here, today.

Nothing was meaningless. Nothing was insignificant. Nothing was a coincidence. Nothing was cliché.

It was all as real as the image of the sea that had outlined my heart one very long night. As real as a delicate, yet firm, seashell.

I jumped again as the image of a tall figure with a Mohawk leapt into my mind and could feel my face, my entire body, playing catch with hot and cold.

"Rebecca?" Adriana eyed me worriedly.

"Water is love," he had said. He was right. I shut my eyes again.

"Would you like to move to the back of the church to talk?" Adriana asked. "I've finished my prayers for now."

I nodded. "Sure."

I grabbed her hand like a small child and quietly pulled her to the back of the church. *A small child who wanted to protect her sister.*

I turned towards Adriana, one thought dominating

all others. "Adri…whatever happened with Robby?"

The surprise evident on Adriana's face told me that the question was not expected. Yet, it also told me, as she stared at her shoes and sighed, that the subject at the center of her maze, her forest, was Robert Donahue.

It also told me something about my own heart…but "what" that was I was not certain.

Or not ready to answer.

"About Robby," Adriana finally looked up and swallowed. She opened her mouth and then closed it, as if uncertain of how to begin.

As well as I knew Adriana—or perhaps because of it—it was sometimes hard to remember that she had been in love before. Perhaps it was also because she had chosen to not talk about it often. I had taken that to mean that she had not wanted to talk about it.

But maybe I had been wrong.

"Does he still write?" I asked quietly.

"Sometimes. There was this long period of time where he didn't…or only sporadically."

My chest burned as she continued.

"You see, we hadn't let on that we…felt that way. Not in so many words, anyway. The official report was that we were just friends. No one made the bold step forward…though I suspect that it slipped out…sometimes."

"Adri, I'm so sorry." My voice couldn't sound as remorseful as my heart. "I should have been there for you. I didn't know how much…" I babbled on futilely.

"No," Adriana interrupted me in the softest tone I had ever heard from her, "I kept it from everyone. I had to…or, at least, I felt that I did. We didn't have a 'summer romance' with kisses and movie nights," she laughed without amusement. "It was a love story that no one would have understood."

"And you still love him."

It wasn't a question. I looked at my friend's pained expression and my eyes became a reflection of her own.

She didn't have to say anything, and she didn't.

But Adriana hadn't finished her story and, after a few moments' pause, she continued.

"We emailed every day for the next year and sent letters in the mail every few weeks," Adriana smiled as she remembered, yet a shadow, cold and dark, covered her wistful eyes.

"But then, suddenly, it stopped. I would hear from him every month, and then every few months. And…" Adriana's voice cracked.

"You don't have to," I said quickly, throwing myself forward to hug her.

"No," Adriana said, waving me away, "I want to."

I moved back.

"And," Adriana continued with more effort, "if it had been because he didn't care anymore, maybe it would have been easier. I wouldn't have been…I wouldn't have been…able to stop loving him at that, but maybe it would have allowed me to…at least give him up…one day. Or maybe the absence of that hope would have made things worse. I don't know. But I knew that…he still cared for me. It came out in the months that he did write. In the birthday cards that he sent. But it was all futile…because he was so far away."

A sob burst forth as Adriana finished, and this time she did not push me away as I leaned forward to hug her.

"But why are you asking about this now?" Adriana asked quizzically, as we moved apart.

I looked at her.

The bells in the front of the church, calling everyone to The Table, rang on cue.

Adriana rushed forward, and I felt the arms of a sister around me.

Chapter Twenty-Eight

Fallitur

"Mr. Asturian!!"

I had captured this moment before...seemingly so long ago, and with a digital camera. But, today, not just two, but dozens of beautiful beach balls splashed with color bounced up and down excitedly about a large net.

The entire religious education classroom was consolidated into one, small corner. *Into an embrace.*

Peter smiled down at the young children crowding around him. They laughed as they tried to move closer for just an inch of him to grasp onto.

They loved him.

I smiled, unable to pull my eyes away from the

scene.

Peter gently moved back to address the crowd. "Boys and girls, I've really enjoyed working with all of you this year. I will miss you."

"I love you," a little girl shyly looked up at Peter with large, expressive eyes. I instantly recognized her as the small child I had been assisting with an illustration during the Family Day celebration right before I had been called away to act as photographer.

"Thank you, Madeleine," Peter smiled at her with affection. "I love you, too. I," he paused, his voice filled with emotion, "love all of you."

"We love you, Mr. Asturian!" the rest of the class chimed in, some teary-eyed, some smiling, some unable to keep still, but all looking at Peter with affection and respect.

The crowd moved closer and, this time, Peter did not move away.

That was…beautiful.

The picturesque scene was interrupted by the sound of a bell. Several audible moans and groans were heard. Peter moved to the front, organizing the class into a neat line, and led them towards the door. Even after every single child was out of the door, he continued to stare at it for several long moments. He finally turned back to me, his eyes misty.

"Hi, Rebecca," he smiled, but it was a tired smile, a defeated smile that I suddenly realized had been there all along, but he had managed to keep from the children. *For their sake.*

He waited, expecting me to finish the customary

greeting. I watched his eyes retreat in weariness and, as I realized yet again with shock, in defeat. Yet, when I opened my mouth, I found that no words came. I closed it quickly and began to stare at the window behind Peter.

I had seen Peter passionately defending his beliefs and scalding evil with his tongue and his pen. I had seen Peter standing quietly, listening, no matter what I had to say, and understanding, no matter how incomprehensible my words. I had seen tenderness, a hint of sadness, when he spoke of his parents and of his beloved home, Alberta. But I had never seen this. I had never seen defeat in his eyes.

And I tasted the defeat, the mixture of despair and bitterness on his countenance, as if it were my own. It hurt me. It hurt me that my rock was hurting almost more than I could bear...so much that I felt a strong resolve deep within me that refused to be ignored.

No matter what his trials entailed, I would not rest until the pain in his eyes turned to laughter.

I finally turned back to Peter, who stood, quietly waiting...as always. He had not moved an inch as far as I could tell. And now, now it was time for me to listen.

I finally opened my mouth again, the words spilling out, "Peter, tell me."

Peter nodded in understanding. He looked down for a long moment, as if undecided as to how to best begin. I waited.

When he finally looked up, I found that he was not looking directly at me, but beyond me. Like I had only a few minutes before, but in a deeper, more lost way. He was traveling to another land. And I knew in my heart that this land was not one of beauty, one of poetic relief.

It was a barren wasteland.

"You probably have wondered what made me come to the U.S.," he said finally in a quiet voice that nevertheless seemed as loud as a thunderstorm in the silence of this small room.

I did not speak, waiting for him to continue.

"It is true that I was impressed by what I had heard of Sacred Heart University. I had always wanted to attend a Catholic school. But there were many great Catholic universities in Alberta, many which I could have enjoyed attending. It is also true that I had always wished to travel, to see the world. But I never expected to be so far away from my family for such an extended period of time. We are," his voice was now barely a whisper, "very close."

He closed his eyes tightly. I wanted to rush over and put my arms around him, to take away his pain. But I held back.

He began again, this time more slowly, "I was in Grade Twelve at Banff High. I was at the top of the world. Not only was the end of high school a month away, but I was a celebrity. I was on the swim team. I had been named one of Banff's top swimmers of all time. We had won nearly every competition that year. And, now, the biggest competition of the season was approaching. We were to face the unbeatable team from a few districts away.

"When I wasn't doing my homework, I was practicing for that competition. My parents suggested that I was working too hard. They told me that I didn't need to win every competition. But I didn't believe them. I worked even harder every time those words were repeated. I wouldn't give up.

"Two days before the competition, Mom and Dad had a business meeting a town away. I was asked to watch over my younger brother, Daniel. I remember the frustration that rose angrily in my chest as they left the house. The competition was so soon. I couldn't afford to lose a single minute.

"I paced back and forth across the house, and finally made a decision. I would go to practice anyway. Dan would be fine. I wouldn't be gone long.

"I considered bringing Dan along, but thought that he would be safer behind a locked door than near a swimming pool when he couldn't swim and I couldn't give him my full attention. I didn't," he swallowed, "want him to drown. I gave him my cell phone number to call if there were any problems, but told him that, if he couldn't get a hold of me because I was in the pool, he could call the next door neighbor. I wrote down both numbers on the back of a piece of paper."

He looked up at me, his eyes hollow. "It wasn't until later that I realized that, on the opposite side of the paper, was a computer-printed picture of the two of us. We were…skiing."

I nodded, unable to speak.

"I set him up with his favorite DVDs. With a quick hug and assurance that I would be back in no time, I left my brother in front of the television set and locked the door. My parents had the family car, so I walked. It didn't matter; school wasn't too far away. I arrived, quickly dashed to the locker room to change into my swimsuit, and hurried to the pool.

"I wasn't sure why I felt the need to hurry. But, once I slipped into the pool, I forgot all about hurrying. I thought that I had all the time in the world. But," he laughed without humor, "this was not a time for Intermission. I practiced my routine over and over again, relaxing into the water, into what had always been my sanctuary. And I forgot about everything else.

"When I arose an hour later, dripping and shivering, from the pool, I knew something was wrong. I ran to my locker, pulling the bag of my regular clothes free. I didn't even bother to put them on. I just ran.

"When I got home," Peter swallowed in recollection, "Dan was gone."

My hand flew to my mouth. *My God…*

"I left the house and searched the entire neighborhood. At the end of my search, on the far end of the street, I found a small shack.

"It was a house that had long been abandoned — about a year after my family and I had moved there — and had fallen into disarray. The windows were broken, as a result of some idle dares made by neighborhood kids back in the day. No one had ever bothered to fix them. Some years later, around when I started high school, I noticed a "No Trespassing" sign on the premises…that, and something else about the place had made me keep my distance.

"But all of that was soon forgotten. Because, there, huddled into a small ball, was my brother.

"I...later found out that he had gotten scared all alone in the house by himself. He missed me and had been trying to find my school when he got lost."

"Was he okay?!" I asked urgently. It was as if I were there, living in the moment. *Living in Peter's past.*

Peter did not speak right away, as if he were confused as to my question, as if he had not heard my words. He stared at the floor.

"He...was okay," he said finally.

"Thank God!" I breathed.

Peter looked up. His eyes were dark and lifeless. "It gets worse."

The look on Peter's face made my heart pound. I blinked back tears.

"It was like a bad movie," he laughed a hollow, empty laugh. "Little Dan ran to me excitedly, bubbling with laughter.

"But that was also when two armed men appeared from out of the shadows, running. And one," his voice was choked with a sob that he could no longer repress, "one pulled the trigger."

I opened my mouth and then closed it. I closed my eyes, not know what to say or what to do. I just stood there, squeezing my eyes shut as the tears swelled in, as the pain of my friend enveloped me.

"It was me that they saw, it was me that they had intended to shoot, if anyone. But it was my brother Dan, my little brother Dan, who was running towards me," he shook his head, "the new...target."

Peter paused. "You see, that shack, the garage of that abandoned house, was the center of a drug ring. Those men were drug dealers. And we were in the wrong place at the wrong time."

He looked at me, his eyes lost and listless. "Cliché?"

I could not hold back any longer. I could not. But I did. I remained still, fixed in the same position, just as Peter was trapped beneath the shadow of his own words.

"But there was a miracle that happened that day. I...certainly didn't deserve it. But God had mercy on my little brother. Little Dan...he...lived. But he didn't live the same way that he had lived before. He lived with the diagnosis that he would never walk again. That...those tiny, beautiful little legs would never again run, never dance, never jump up and down with the bright smile of youth. Never."

"No," I said, my heart caught in my throat, "you never know what—"

Peter waved my words aside. "I know. But somehow...somehow that doesn't..."

He stopped, unable to speak, and we both stood there, together, in silence.

When he spoke again, he sounded much older, his voice even more weary than before.

"You see," he said finally, his eyes blind with tears, "this time...this time, my brother was the Intermission. He was the one that...mattered. He was—"

"The space between the notes," I finished softly.

Peter nodded, a slow, slight movement. "I...didn't want to let down my team, but I ended up letting down my brother. Letting him down in a way that was…indelible."

He paused for a moment before continuing.

"There was a court case which we won, but there was still tension in the air. My parents told me that they wanted me to get an education away from all of this, to…make something of myself far away from everything. And," he shifted his feet, "although they never spoke words of blame to me, I think that it was hard for them to have me there, too."

No, Peter. They loved you. They love you.

"I argued with them. I told them that I had caused this, that I should put off school and get a job right away to help with the medical bills, that," his voice grew strained, "I had to be there for Dan. Little Dan."

I wanted to protest, to shout, to tell Peter that it was not his fault, that it had been an accident. But, once again, I stood, immobile, transfixed, unable to move.

"For a year and a half, I worked full-time and took night classes at the local community college. But eventually I did as they asked. I think I convinced myself that it would be better for my parents that way…so that they wouldn't have to see me, to be reminded of the person responsible for—" he stopped abruptly, but there was no need to continue. I knew what would follow.

"And," he shook his head, a sad shadow of a smile playing ironically on his lips, "here I am…with *children*. Sweet, beautiful children who I have no right to be near. Sometimes, when…I miss Alberta, when I hurt, hurt about anything, they bring joy to my life. But I have no right to have that joy, Rebecca." His voice grew even more hollow than it had yet. "I…destroyed one of them…the one who mattered the most in the world to me. Another angel should not lose its wings because of *these*," he moved his hands frenetically, his voice growing louder, shaking, fighting against the trembling that shook his body, "hands."

And I could be silent no longer.

"No, Peter," I said. "You are a teacher. A *teacher*. A father. A father to these," I pointed at the door where the young students had left seemingly so long ago, "children, and one who will be a father to many others in the future." My voice was cracking, but I refused to stop, "A heart larger than that of any teacher that I know, of any teacher who holds a piece of paper saying that he can teach or a diploma announcing the completion of his degree. And brilliance and thoughtfulness of mind and spirit. And a soul, a spirit, filled with the Light of Christ."

A glance at the surprised expression on Peter's face made me realize that I had been yelling. There was a pause, a silence, but my eyes refused to leave him, filled with the newly-arisen resolve of my tongue.

The corner of Peter's mouth moved slightly and he finally spoke.

"Thank you," he said softly.

"Thank you for everything," I said in response, staring at Peter's eyebrow on the one day that his eyes would not address mine.

He shrugged his shoulders almost casually, as if nothing crucial had transpired. Yet I knew him too well. The action was too deliberate and unnatural. It was forced. And his eyes—his eyes betrayed him.

"I didn't do anything," he said.

"Yes…yes, you did." My pen was fiercely writing, a battle that I obstinately refused to lose. It must have reached my eyes because I saw its effect on those of Peter. His eyes once again showed surprise, but there was also an emotion in them that I did not wish to name.

Sadness. Sadness in a dear, sweet, wonderful, *beautiful* kindred spirit whom I never, ever wanted to see hurt, see in such pain, such agony, see suffering.

But there was yet another emotion in those great eyes of his. An emotion that I could not name. The expression of his eyes had so often wrapped around me, held me close in a true embrace, when it seemed that some reserve held back his arms. His eyes could not be restrained, and I suddenly came to understand that he had never wanted to keep that from me, even if he were able. And I realized that, although it was such an inherent characteristic of Peter, it could not be duplicated in its entirety to each and every human being. *Peter and me.*

"High five," Peter said quietly. "You probably wondered why I held back. Little Dan and I…he would always jump up and give me a high five when I got home from school."

Oh, Peter.

"And that day we went to the Adoration Chapel…it was the anniversary of my brother's…accident. I…needed it as much as you did."

He remained, unflinching, with that never-changing, ever-fixed gaze returning to his countenance, returning to him.

But it was not enough.

"Peter, you are...my rock," I said softly.

I could restrain myself no longer. I threw my arms around him. I closed my eyes as they, once again, grew unfocused and blurry. When some time later—after what felt like an eternity, an eternity in which healing washed over two huddled forms—I reluctantly drew back, I saw that his eyes, too, were moist. And they still held mine.

"You've been such a blessing in my life...thank you," he said simply.

"You are my rock," I repeated, managing to choke out the words.

And then I suddenly remembered.

I hoped that he understood Spanish. His occasional usage of well-known Spanish words and phrases did not mean that he had studied the language. I had always forgotten to ask. But the poem had wanted to be written in Spanish, and there was nothing that I could have done about it. I had had no choice but to listen.

"You are my rock...with a porthole," I added.

He looked at me quizzically and then, slowly, beautifully, and fully, a brilliant smile began to spread across his face.

"Oh, yeah. I saw one of those on August 25, 2004."

The room, from the large white board to the smallest scrap of paper lying idly, long forgotten, on one of the children's desks, soon rang with a laughter that could not, and never would be, contained.

Peter told me that he had returned to Alberta, Canada because the case involving his brother and the drug dealers had been reopened. It seemed that the drug dealers had claimed that Peter had been responsible for the accident, that they had new evidence that would reveal that Peter had shot his own brother. He was not able to tell me any more due to the confidentiality of the case. I shook my head, horrified and angry, but assured Peter that such lies would ultimately not stand up to the justice of God's Law. He nodded slowly, and admitted that, so far, the case was going in his favor.

With all of the calamity and chaos that had transpired, he had not had time to even touch a computer. He had not checked his email.

He had never received the emails that I had sent him.

"I'm sorry," he said, looking searchingly into my eyes for my reaction. "I should have told you before I left. I was just…not myself. It all happened so quickly. I first heard about it the morning of Family Day."

I nodded. "I noticed that you weren't yourself that day."

"I saw that."

"But, please," I shook my head, waving away his apology, "there is no need to apologize."

Peter had smiled, shaking his head. "You are a

blessing. And…you were right when you said that…there were no coincidences. There really aren't."

I nodded, smiling, unable to say a word.

I also learned that he was to leave for Alberta the very next day…and, this time, to stay.

Due to the inconvenience of the court session, his flight had been paid by the court in order to allow time for goodbyes and any unfinished business in America. He would spend the remainder of Easter Sunday with his family, and was expected to be back in the courthouse on Monday.

Time for goodbyes. *Time.*

One day.

I was once again caught speechless. I wanted to cry, but, this time, for his sake, I restrained myself.

"May God be with you…always," I finally managed to say.

"And with you, Rebecca." He looked at me, his eyes once again sad.

No. No more sadness.

I reminded him with a smile to read the poem. He promised that he would, telling me that he could not wait to see what his favorite author had cooked up this time. I nodded, fishing in my pocket to hand him the palm cross that I had made for him seemingly so long ago. He received it, holding it in the palm of his hand for several moments without saying a word. He finally placed it gently in his pocket, looking up with a brilliant, iridescent smile. *With Peter's smile.* My eyebrows creased together in emotion. I couldn't do this.

But I had to.

And, when he left the room, when our final goodbyes were all that remained in the waiting pulse of air and sky, I stood, once again immobile. After he left, my eyes glued to the door, I suddenly realized that I had not completed the customary farewell for someone you may not see again..."Don't forget me," or, perhaps, "Remember to write."

Perhaps that meant something. Perhaps two kindred spirits could never truly be apart.

I knew that he would not forget me. I just knew...just as I knew that I would never forget him. Nor would I ever forget to think of him. As Anne Shirley of Prince Edward Island once said, long ago in Lucy Maud Montgomery's fictional world, "True friends are always together in spirit."

And he would write. I knew that he would write.

I reached into my old, silver purse.

The purse that had lived through so much in just the last month and a half.

My hand caught hold of a familiar shape. I took out my inhaler, now with more acceptance than distaste, yet, as I did, I found that it was not alone. In the process of removing the machine, a small, golden piece of paper had slid on top of it.

One word. *Intermission.*

Tears streamed down my face as I stared at the piece of paper for several moments. I held it tightly in my hand as if embracing an old friend.

One day.

One day of forty.

My hand finally lost its firm grip and, lifting the paper to my face, I kissed it lightly before returning it to my purse.

"Goodbye," I whispered.

With inhaler in hand, I walked to my parents' room.

Mom was standing in front of the mirror, placing a sticky note against its reflective surface, a characteristic element of her reminder system.

"Mom?"

She turned towards me inquisitively. "What's up?"

"Could you help me with my inhaler?"

Mom put down her notepad. "Rebecca, you know how to use it."

"I know. But...could you still help me with it?"

Mom looked at me for one long moment.

"Of course."

I walked to her, holding out the inhaler. She took it, shaking the canister and then reinserting it into the aero chamber.

I leaned forward as she pressed down on the medicine tube.

1001

Peter.

1002

I will never forget you. Never.

1003

Beautiful.

1004
All is calm, all is bright.
1005
Adoro te devote.
1006
I thirst.

SCENE 17

In an Auditorium:

Four individuals stand huddled behind a large, red curtain. They are excited, yet nervous. It is the night of the first performance of MUSE: THE PLAY. The beginning is only moments away. **Morena**, **Monet**, **Antonio**, *and* **Elise** *pause to reflect.*

Monet [briskly]: Well, what matters is that it is done.

Antonio [confidently]: Or, perhaps, that we wrote it.

Elise [smiles at Antonio, blushing]: Together.

Morena [thoughtfully, with a smile]: Or, maybe

what really mattered was that game of Crazy 8s.

The four individuals, so different yet alike, laugh together as good friends. The curtain opens. The play is about to begin.

Or, perhaps, *continue.*

And no one knew what the intermission of the play would bring…

Chapter Twenty-Nine

Sed

It was Easter.

40 Days.

Cedric handed me the basket with a smile, and I remembered.

♪ *Somewhere in between my heart and the highest star in the heavens, the angels gather 'round to sing Your praise… And I am blest. I am blest. I am blest…just to think that I could offer You my song while the angels sing along.* ♪

The waves of the great sea, now a song, shone forth.

A song. A story.

In that moment, all of my memories came forward and became that moment. *Déjà vu.* Yet that moment was greater than the sum of its parts.

It was the Everything that I knew.

I traced my hand along the contours of an emerald rose, a maze of mazes that lay in my outstretched hand.

Once, long ago, I had looked at Peter and Cedric and imagined that I saw a shepherd guiding its flock. I had wondered which one of them was the sheep and which the shepherd. I realized now, as I returned Cedric's smile, that they were neither. They were both a bit of each...guided by the Greatest Shepherd of Them All.

The woman to the right of me, a familiar face fringed by fiery red locks, took the basket from me, passing on the smile.

Nothing was a coincidence. Nothing was irrelevant.

Cedric moved on to the next row, the joy of Easter reaching his eyes. *Fred forever marked on his countenance.*

Our unfinished Intermission. Incomplete, but hopeful. The story that Peter and I had set out so eagerly to write waited, quietly. Beginning, middle, and end, known in part, yet unknown in fullness.

An intermission that would never end. An intermission of hope.

I closed my eyes and drank in the fullness of the moment.

Writing was a circular process, I realized, *not linear like many believed*. We wrote what we were called to write at the moment, regardless of the chronological order.

What we were called to write.

Nothing was a coincidence. Nothing was irrelevant.

"Intuition is the space between your thoughts,"

Father D'Angelo said softly, looking at the congregation, looking within the congregation, looking straight at me.

I paused, recalling something.

Music was the space between the notes.

And I realized that these Sundays of Lent had been just that. *The space between the notes.* A time in which true meaning was found.

Sundays of Lent, moments of innocence, glimpses of hope.

The freedom of the swings, the laughter of trust, the dreams of forests long asleep.

Baila.

A dance, a song.

The simple was the most complex, the complex the most simple. The little events were always the big ones.

The never-ending stretch of sea and sand.

I looked at the family gathered around me...my brother, temporarily subdued, my mother, singing joyfully, and my father, peace in his eyes. And the family beyond, Peter in my heart, Cedric in my vision, Adriana in front of me, my grandparents beside me, all those who had gathered together to celebrate Christ's Resurrection surrounding me.

On the contrary, everyone is here.

I smiled, and felt peace deep within my heart.

Mi concha de mar
Escrito por Rebecca
para Peter

Bajo las olas del mar
Están escritos muchos tesoros
Las curvas misteriosas del galán
El caballito de mar.
Polvo delicado de hadas
Tejido en los hilos
De un tapiz encantado
El brillo de piedras ancianas
Pero sin agujero de Libertad
Para permitir entrar El Sol.
Sólo roza la superficie.

Pero cuando el marinero
Pasa en su barco
Y la brisa del mar
De su alrededor
Como indagadores insistentes
Que buscan tesoro más brillante
Sin duda encuentran
La concha de mar.

Esta concha de mar
Vive en un mar de lejos
Pero se acerca a la orilla
Cuando respiran las olas
De risa o llanto
De sol o lluvia

O nada en particular.

Por dentro se puede oír
La canción del mar
Refleja cada ola
Pero es única.
Caballero de la corte
Sabio como si refleje
Cada estrato y color
Que Dios la dio.
Firme por fuera
Pero con entrada de Libertad
Dispuesta para recibir
La amistad.
Un espíritu noble
Un pedazo del mar.

Epilogue

"And here we are," I waved with my free hand, as if he could see it. "*Hundreds* of ducks...okay, okay, maybe dozens. But, regardless, they're *here*. Browns and grays and whites...some with green. I *still* haven't figured out which are male and which are female..."

I paused, gazing at my surroundings. It was a bright, sunny day at the city park, and something akin to sanctuary wove its way through the light breeze rippling across my dark locks. "And the water is just...*sparkling*. The sun is reflecting off of it and," I heaved a great sigh, "it's just so *beautiful*, Peter. I wish you could see it."

"I do, too," said a quiet voice on the other end.

"And so you shall!" I said, determined, "as

promised!"

"Thank you. And one day, one day, perhaps I will. I hope."

"As do I."

"After all, Intermission has just begun."

"Exactly! And...eww!"

"What?" The voice rose in anticipation as I grasped my phone more tightly. *Silly me.* I had almost dropped the thing in surprise.

"There are, like, ten really creepy little black birds with red eyes and they look like Sith Lords," I rushed in a single breath.

A deep chuckle resonated from the other end of the phone.

I smiled. *Oh, how I had missed that laugh.* The past year had seemed more like twenty.

"And one just approached my right flip-flop."

"Oh, no!"

"But, do not fear!" I proclaimed. "I have brought sufficient weaponry." I balanced my cell phone carefully against one ear as I unzipped my purse. "The ever so valiant...windshield wipers!"

"But, of course!"

"Dude, is that a goose?!"

"I have...no idea."

"And there is an adorable bunny peeking out from amongst the underbrush. Aww, the psycho Sith Lords must have scared her."

"Undoubtedly."

"And look! Uh, I mean...listen!" I laughed. This long distance communication still took some getting used to. "It may please you to know that I have just spotted a rather large Redwood tree, which, quite obviously, is the one that sheltered Antonio and Monet during a rather lively game of Crazy 8's."

"But, of course."

I paused. "Someone obviously removed their table. How rude!"

"*Most* rude!"

I nodded and, then, with a laugh, expressed the action verbally.

"Just remember to watch out for the bees, Rebecca."

"As Adriana would say, 'duly noted'."

"Good."

I squinted, looking farther ahead. *There it was.* A large grin quickly spread across my face.

"But, we have yet to experience the climax of Intermission."

I ran, firmly holding onto my phone, but *free.*

Ever so free.

I ran, peals of laughter resonating far, far away to Alberta, Canada.

I ran, knowing my destination, but not knowing, never knowing, what was in store.

I caught hold of the silver chain and smiled. "Ready to swing, Peter?"

Appendix

Dear Reader:

Please remember that no language may be directly translated into another. The full meaning is often lost; this is one example.

- R.E.V.

Mi concha de mar	My Seashell
Escrito por Rebecca	*Written by Rebecca*
para Peter	*For Peter*

Bajo las olas del mar	Beneath the waves of the sea
Están escritos muchos tesoros	Are written many treasures
Las curvas misteriosas del galán	The mysterious curves of the hero
El caballito de mar.	The starfish.
Polvo delicado de hadas	Delicate fairy dust
Tejido en los hilos	Woven in the threads
De un tapiz encantado	Of an enchanted tapestry
El brillo de piedras ancianas	The brilliance of ancient stones
Pero sin agujero de Libertad	But without an opening of Liberty
Para permitir entrar El Sol.	To allow entrance of the sun.
Sólo roza la superficie.	It only scrapes the surface.
Pero cuando el marinero	But when the sailor
Pasa en su barco	Passes in his ship
Y la brisa del mar	And the breeze of the sea
De su alrededor	Around it
Como indagadores insistentes	Like insistent inspectors
Que buscan tesoro más brillante	That search for a more brilliant treasure
Sin duda encuentran	Without a doubt they will find
La concha de mar.	The seashell.
Esta concha de mar	This seashell
Vive en un mar de lejos	Lives in a faraway sea
Pero se acerca a la orilla	But moves closer to the coast
Cuando respiran las olas	When the waves breathe
De risa o llanto	Of laughter or tears
De sol o lluvia	Of the sun or the rain
O nada en particular.	Or nothing in particular.
Por dentro se puede oír	Inside (the shell) may be heard
La canción del mar	The song of the sea
Refleja cada ola	It reflects each wave
Pero es única.	But remains unique.
Caballero de la corte	Knight of the Court
Sabio como si refleje	Wise as if it reflects
Cada estrato y color	Each layer and color
Que Dios la dio.	That God gave it.
Firme por fuera	Firm on the outside
Pero con entrada de Libertad	But with an opening of Freedom
Dispuesta para recibir	Ready to receive
La amistad.	Friendship.
Un espíritu noble	A noble spirit
Un pedazo del mar.	A piece of the sea.

Lo inmortal	The Immortal
Escrito por Rebecca	*Written by Rebecca*
Las hojas pintadas de rojo vuelan	The leaves painted red fly
Sin moverse de su santuario.	Without moving from their sanctuary
Un paso las marca por muerte	A step marks them for death
Y quedan inmaculadas sin arruga.	And they remain untouched.
Llaman al viento del viejo	They call the wind of an ancient
ayer	yesterday
Pero siempre están en el presente	But they are always in the present
Y sin duda quedan inscritas	And, without a doubt, remain inscribed
En la larga noche del futuro.	In the long night of the future.
El color brillante sonríe	The brilliant color smiles
Con la suave sutileza del amanecer	With the soft gentleness of dawn
Un nuevo comienzo que ya había nacido	A new beginning that has just been born
Hace una indeleble eternidad.	Since an indelible eternity.
Ninguna hoja es idéntica	No leaf is identical
No conoce el mismo tono.	They do not know the same shade
El rojo de alba	The red of dawn
Y el rojo de crepúsculo	And the red of twilight
La llegada y la salida.	The arrival and the departure
Como sus compañeros del libro	Like their companions of the book
Uno nunca parece como el anterior	One is never identical to the previous
Pero conoce el mismo aire.	But knows the same air
Hay tantas hojas que vuelan	There are many leaves that fly
Sin moverse de su santuario.	Without moving from their sanctuary.
Y el vuelo continúa sin	And the flight continues without
empezar.	beginning.

Acknowledgements

First and foremost, I thank God for the gifts—especially Love—that He has bestowed upon me. This story would not be possible without Him.

I would like to thank my mother, Jackie Marinello-Sweeney, who was one of the very first readers of *I Thirst*. Thank you for believing in me and my story, but also providing honest criticism. My love of reading was inspired by your own. Thank you for introducing me to the fantastical world of fairy tales, a world that still influences me today. Most of all, thank you for loving me with the heart of a true mother.

To my father, Larry Sweeney, for your storytelling. I will never forget how, when I was little, we would tell each other stories, alternating back and forth until The

End. It may be a long time since the days of "Captain Hook Goes to the Dentist," but I still appreciate it. Thank you for being a wonderful father…as well as the arch nemesis in any game of Crazy 8's.

To my brother, Vincent Marinello-Sweeney, for your randomness and creativity. We may be getting older, but, to me, you will always be my comrade in those imagination games of "Spies" and "Peter Pan and Winnie the Pooh." Thank you for the goofy moments and for always entertaining us with your sci-fi character impressions. Thank you for being the best big brother in the world. For the record, I still think you should build a spaceship.

Thank you to my grandparents, Arthur and Vera Marinello, for your unending love, generosity, and encouragement. Thank you, Grandpa, for 'getting' the poet in me. It is truly wonderful to be able to have a "writer's conversation" with someone so dear to me. Thank you, Grandma, for teaching me how to read. I do not know where I would be without a book in my hand. Thank you also for encouraging me to get published. Perhaps one day that children's book will materialize.

I would like to thank those wonderful kindred spirits that I call friends. Your encouragement throughout the writing, editing, and publication processes has meant the world to me. I would especially like to thank those friends who know the true meaning of random insanity and for the circle of writers, past and present, who have always supported, encouraged, and understood.

To my teachers and professors who encouraged me to keep writing, thank you. I truly appreciate it.

In memory of Msgr. Gus Moretti, who baptized me into the faith, and Msgr. Joe George, who defined my childhood. Through you and others was made visible the Light of Christ. Msgr. Moretti, I may not remember you well, but I need only turn to my grandfather, your close friend, or look at the video of my baptism to see that you were truly a special person and a great soul. Msgr. Joe, I so wish you were here to see *I Thirst* in print. I cannot tell you how much I miss you. Yet, as I write, I can almost see you smiling in Heaven. Thank you for being our dear family friend and, even more, *family*. You will never be forgotten.

To Jansina of Rivershore Books, thank you for your hard work, encouragement, and support. I feel so blessed to have been given the opportunity to work with you. Thank you for believing in me and taking a chance on my story. Most of all, thank you for wanting to stay up late to read my book.

To Ray McBride for the beautiful photos that grace the cover of *I Thirst*. Thank you for your assistance, kindness, and support. Most of all, thank you for caring about lighthouses as much as I do.

To Lucia Zinkewich for introducing me to the beautiful prayer, "Adoro Te Devote." This story would not be the same without it. Thank you for your support, friendship, and prayers.

And to that random guy at Mass who looked like a sea captain—I don't know who you are, but thank you.

Author Bio

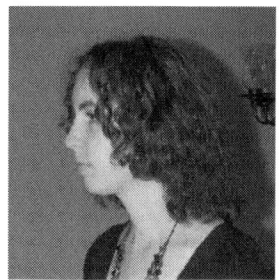 Gina Marinello-Sweeney has been writing ever since she was a little girl and turned her bedroom into a "library," complete with due date slips and a check-out stamp. As her own stories were "checked out" by family and friends, she dreamed of a day in which her stories would be available in public libraries worldwide. Her dream of publication came true in 2013. Gina is also an avid poet in both the English and Spanish languages. In 2009, she was asked to present some original Spanish poems at an international literature conference in Costa Rica. Although unable to attend this event, a presentation of the poems was well-received at another scholarly event that same year. Graduating summa cum laude, Gina completed a degree in liberal studies, an elementary school teaching credential, and a minor in Spanish. In her spare time, she enjoys producing videos, going to the beach, reading, and traveling. Gina lives in southern California, where she is at work on the sequel to *I Thirst*, as well as the first book in a fantasy series.

Visit www.ginamarinellosweeney.com for more information.

Rivershore Books

Website: www.rivershorebooks.com
Blog: www.rivershorebooks.blogspot.com
Forum: rivershorebooks.proboards.com
Facebook: www.facebook.com/rivershorebooks
Email: Jansina@rivershorebooks.com

Printed in Poland
by Amazon Fulfillment
Poland Sp. z o.o., Wrocław